"The ba...
she...

"Have at it," he said. "Bathing babies is not my department."

"And why not?" she said, folding her arms and tapping her foot.

A fighting stance if he'd ever seen one. He held up his hands. "These hands strip rifles and change flat tires and chop wood and put worms on hooks. Men things."

She was looking at his hands with a strange hunger burning in her eyes, a hunger that made him realize his hands wanted to explore all kinds of softer territory.

"It's a two-person job," she said firmly. "Wet babies are slippery."

He knew, suddenly, that just as he had helped her face the challenge of her fears, she was now asking him to explore new territory, move out of his comfort zone.

"I've already found out all about slippery babies."

"Well, then this should be a piece of cake for you, Major."

Dear Reader,

Baby birds are chirping, bees are buzzing and the tulips are beginning to bud. Spring is here, so why not revive the winter-weary romantic in you by reading four brand-new love stories from Silhouette Romance this month.

What's an old soldier to do when a bunch of needy rug rats and a hapless beauty crash his retreat? Fall in love, of course! Follow the antics of this funny little troop in *Major Daddy* (#1710) by Cara Colter.

In *Dylan's Last Dare* (#1711), the latest title in Patricia Thayer's dynamite THE TEXAS BROTHERHOOD miniseries, a cranky cowboy locks horns with his feisty physical therapist and then learns she has a little secret she soon won't be able to hide!

Jordan Bishop wants to dwell in a castle and live happily ever after, but somehow things aren't going as she's planned, in *An Heiress on His Doorstep* (#1712) by Teresa Southwick. This is the final title in Southwick's delightful IF WISHES WERE…miniseries in which three friends have their dreams come true in unexpected ways.

When a bookworm meets her prince and discovers she's a real-life princess, will she be able to make her own happy ending? Find out in *The Secret Princess* (#1713) by Elizabeth Harbison.

Celebrate the new season, feel the love and join in the fun by experiencing each of these lively new love stories from Silhouette Romance!

Mavis C. Allen
Associate Senior Editor

Please address questions and book requests to:
Silhouette Reader Service
U.S.: 3010 Walden Ave., P.O. Box 1325, Buffalo, NY 14269
Canadian: P.O. Box 609, Fort Erie, Ont. L2A 5X3

Major Daddy

CARA COLTER

SILHOUETTE *Romance*®

Published by Silhouette Books

America's Publisher of Contemporary Romance

For those courageous women who love the men—
sons, brothers, husbands, fathers—
who go to war

SILHOUETTE BOOKS

ISBN 0-373-19710-1

MAJOR DADDY

Copyright © 2004 by Cara Colter

This edition published by arrangement with Harlequin Books S.A.

® and TM are trademarks of Harlequin Books S.A., used under license.
Trademarks indicated with ® are registered in the United States Patent
and Trademark Office, the Canadian Trade Marks Office and in other
countries.

Visit Silhouette at www.eHarlequin.com

Printed in U.S.A.

Books by Cara Colter

CARA COLTER

shares ten acres in the wild Kootenay region of British Columbia with the man of her dreams, three children, two horses, a cat with no tail and a golden retriever who answers best to "bad dog." She loves reading, writing and the woods in winter (no bears). She says life's delights include an automatic garage door opener and the skylight over the bed that allows her to see the stars at night.

She also says, "I have not lived a neat and tidy life, and used to envy those who did. Now I see my struggles as having given me a deep appreciation of life, and of love, that I hope I succeed in passing on through the stories that I tell."

MAJOR COLE STANDEN'S SURVIVAL STRATEGY

(for handling emergencies when stranded with five children, one wounded senior citizen and a beautiful woman)

CODE YELLOW
Diaper change, liquid variety.
Emergency rating: minor.

CODE BROWN
Diaper change, horrible variety.
Clothespins and/or face mask may be required.
Emergency rating: moderate.

CODE RED
Brooke Callan. Beautiful, bossy and armed with Mace. Be alert for the heart to do strange things when she's in the vicinity.
Emergency rating: major.

Prologue

Cole Standen woke with a start. For a moment, in the inky, impenetrable darkness, he thought he was in that inhospitable land of icy-cold nights, blowing sand, ragged, rocky places and hidden dangers. The blood surged and his muscles tensed, battle alert, ready. He held his breath, listening.

It was the scent that brought him back to reality. The aroma of cedar and pine, made richer by the dampness in the storm-tossed night, rushed in the open bedroom window and comforted him. It was the smell of his boyhood.

And then he became aware of the sounds outside the shelter of the sturdy cabin. The wind was savage, howling through the treetops. Rain hammered the metal roof. Waves crashed and rolled on the rock-lined shore of the lake.

He sighed and felt his muscles relax. He remembered he was home.

His eyes adjusted minutely to the murky darkness and

the rough log walls of his bedroom came into focus. The mattress beneath him was firm and comfortable, a plaid bedroom-window curtain flapped and jigged with the wind.

He had gone to sleep with the wind high—raising the waves to ferocious whitecaps on the lake, swaying the treetops, shrieking through the soffit under the eaves—so he knew the wind had not woken him.

Cole had a soldier's gift for sifting out those noises that were supposed to be there—no matter how chaotic—and sleeping through them with relative ease. But something out of the ordinary, no matter how small, could bring him instantly awake. The sound he thought he had heard was so fragile, so tiny, it was easy to believe he had imagined it.

He waited under the comfortable weight of a down comforter for his sense of safety to return, for his mind to sound the all clear.

He reminded himself that he was virtually alone here at this isolated bay on Kootenay Lake, an enormous body of water located in the shadows of British Columbia's Purcell Mountains. Unlike most men, he craved solitude and found solace in it.

It was November. The summer people had boarded up the windows of the rare cabins that dotted the inlet and had gone home long ago.

Only the new house—rumored to be a movie star's—showed signs of occupation. He had noticed fresh tire tracks on the impossibly steep driveway. At night, light spilled from windows of the house high on the point and wove ribbons of gold into the black, restless water beyond the bay.

The new house was a monstrosity of tasteless white stucco that had changed the landscape of Heartbreak Bay forever, and that Cole heartily resented every time he caught a glimpse of it. Still, it was a long distance up the bay, far enough away that his sense of isolation remained safely intact.

Despite how his reasoning mind tried to tell him he was as safe here as he could ever be anywhere, Cole's deeper mind—that place of pure instinct that had kept him alive so many times—did not sound the all clear. Cole frowned, and then he heard it, suddenly, again.

His frown deepened, and he reached for the light beside his bed. The lamp clicked but did not come on. No power, not an unusual situation in this remote bay that was subjected to cruel weather from November until February. He reached for the flashlight on his night table and played the beam across the ceiling. The light did not persuade him that he had not heard a sound, frail and pitiful, like the mewing of a kitten.

Restless now, Cole threw back the covers, yanked on a pair of jeans, and went and stood at the window. The air was biting against his naked chest.

Tap. Tap. Tap. The hair on the back of his neck rose. The noise was puny, almost lost in the furor of the storm, and yet there it was again. *Tap. Tap. Tap.*

He followed the sound out of his bedroom, following the beam of his flashlight over rough hardwood floors, past the ragtag collection of cabin furniture in the living room.

Tap. Tap. Tap.

The sound was on the other side of the front door. He told himself a tree branch must be scraping it. He reminded himself he was home, in Canada, safe, and yet it was a warrior who flung open the door, ready and fierce.

At first he saw only the night, felt the sting of rain

against his face and the cold fingers of wind in his hair. But then that small sound, the kitten mewing, made him look down, and his flashlight beam illuminated a most startling sight.

His jaw dropped.

A small girl stood there, her white nightdress whipping around her, a doll wrapped in a bright blanket clutched tight to her chest.

Perhaps eleven, the child was painfully thin, and her long dark hair tangled, curly, around her head. Her eyes were huge and blue and frightened, and her teeth were chattering. A fine line of blue was appearing around her lips despite the sweater pulled over the nightdress.

The doll she was holding suddenly let out a fierce yell, as frightening as any battle cry Cole had ever heard. He took an alarmed step back and scrutinized the bundle the girl held.

It squirmed, and he realized it was not a doll. It was a baby! His blood went cold, and his mind tried to sort through the hodgepodge of illogical information that was being thrust on it.

The soldier, the commander, stepped in coolly and took charge. It told him job one was to get these kids out of the cold. No matter how startling their appearance on his doorstep, there would be time, later, to sort through the intrigues.

"Get in," he ordered and was stunned when the child hesitated before the authority in his voice, a voice that men raced to obey.

He saw suddenly her arms were trembling from the effort of holding the baby, and firmly, a soldier doing the thing he least wanted to do, but recognizing his lack of choices, he plucked the baby from her arms.

It stared at him with huge blue eyes just like the girl's

and screwed up its face until the eyes disappeared into a nest of wrinkles. But then, mercifully, instead of crying the baby nestled into him, sighed, plopped a plump thumb into its mouth.

''Come in,'' he said, again, trying to take the military snap out of his voice, trying for a note of kindness that might reassure the trembling waif before him.

She regarded him with huge eyes that stripped him to his soul, and then gave a small satisfied nod. But still, she did not step over the threshold to warmth and safety.

She turned on the step and motioned with her arm. A motion any soldier would recognize.

Come forward. The shrubs that formed a border around the small square of yard that surrounded the house, parted.

Cole almost dropped the baby. A toddler, not more than three, obviously female from the foolishness of the lace-trimmed nightdress that tangled around pudgy legs, emerged from the shrubs and tottered across the leaf-and branch-strewn yard.

As if he was not reeling from enough shock, the shrubs parted again, and two small boys, maybe seven and eight, dark-haired, dirt-smeared and pajama-clad, also emerged into the clearing of his cabin.

Cole Standen had faced the types of terror that make a man tremble and reach inside himself to find his deepest reserves of courage.

He had jumped from airplanes, been shot at, dealt with the dread of an enemy concealed by night but so close you could almost feel his breath upon your cheek.

But as those cold, wet, mud-spattered children tumbled by him into his sanctuary, and the warm puddle of humanity that was the baby squirmed against his bare chest, Cole searched his memory bank to see if he had ever faced a terror quite like the one that hammered in his breast now.

He discovered he had not.

Chapter One

"My granny's dead," the girl, obviously the oldest of the five, announced. And then, her bravery all used up, her face crumpled as if the air was being let out of a balloon. She began to cry, quietly at first, big silent tears rolling down her face. The silence was but the still before the storm. She built quickly to a crescendo. She uttered a heartbreaking wail.

The four other waifs watched her anxiously, and her breakdown was a lesson in leadership. All four of them instantly followed her example. Even the baby. They screwed up their faces in expressions of identical distress and began to caterwaul. Awkwardly gripping the baby, which seemed unaccountably slippery, Cole escorted the four other howling children into his living room and planted them on the couch.

The older girl held out her arms, and he carefully placed the screaming baby back in her care. All the children huddled together in a messy pile of tangled limbs and wept until their skinny shoulders heaved and their sobs were interspersed with hiccups.

Cole did not know very much about children, but he hoped hiccup-crying did not induce vomiting.

Quickly, he checked the phone—which naturally was out—stoked the fire and lit his two coal-oil lamps.

He turned back and studied the children in the flickering yellow light. He realized he was in trouble. The crying continued unabated—in fact it seemed to be rising in tempo and intensity. He had no doubt the children were going to make themselves sick if they continued. There was also the possibility that grandma—wherever she was—might not be dead and might urgently require his assistance.

He held up a hand. "Hey," he said, in his best commander voice, "that's enough."

There was momentary silence while they all gazed wide-eyed at his raised hand, and then one of them whimpered and the rest of them dissolved all over again.

He clapped his hands. He stamped his foot. He roared.

And nothing worked, until something divine whispered in his ear what was required to stop the noise and squeeze the story out of the little mites.

Surrender.

The soldier in him resisted. Surrender? It was not in his vocabulary. But he resisted only momentarily. The noise and emotion in the room were going to send him on a one-way trip into the lake if it didn't stop.

So, summoning all his courage, he took the baby back, discovered why she seemed unaccountably slippery and did his best to ignore it. He wedged himself a spot on the couch between the children. Blessed and stunned silence followed while the little troop evaluated this latest development. And then, before Cole could really prepare himself properly, the two boys and the toddler in the ridiculous dress were all vying for a place on his lap— and found it. The older girl snuggled in so tight under his arm it felt as if she was crushing his heart.

The combined weight of the children and the baby was startlingly small. It was their warmth that surprised him, the seeming bonelessness of them as they melted into him, like kittens who had found a mother.

For an old soldier, a terrifying thing happened.

Soaked in tears and whatever horrible warm liquid that was seeping out of the baby's diaper, he felt a terrible weakness, a softening around his heart.

"Okay," he said, putting his voice into the blessed silence with extreme caution, "tell me what happened to Grandma." Out of the sudden chorus of overlapping voices, he began to pick out a story.

"The lights went out."

"She fell down the steps."

"Blood everywhere."

"Lots of blood. Maybe bwains, too."

In bits and pieces, like putting together a verbal jigsaw puzzle, Cole figured out who the children were, where they were from and what needed to be done.

They were the movie star's children. When the power had gone out, their grandma, who looked after them when their mother was away, had fallen down the steps in the darkness. The children had presumed, erroneously, Cole hoped, that she was dead.

"I knew I had to get help," the oldest girl told him solemnly, "but they—" she stabbed an accusing finger at the two boys "—said they had to come, too. And we couldn't leave Kolina—"

"That me," the toddler in the dress told him, then

relaxed into his chest, her cheek warm and soft and wet, and inserted her thumb in her mouth.

"—or the baby, so we all came. And here we are, Mr. Herman."

Mr. Herman? They obviously had him confused with a different neighbor, possibly one who was friendly.

He considered telling them he was not Mr. Herman, but they had a shell-shocked look about them that told him to save his breath.

He saw immediately the order of things that needed to be done. He had to get to the grandma and fast. Possibly, she was not dead, but hovering on the brink, where seconds could count.

"Your name?" he demanded of the oldest one.

"Saffron," she told him, and the rest of them piped up with the most bewildering and ridiculous assortment of names he'd ever heard. The older of the boys was Darrance, and the other one was Calypso. Calypso!

The smallest girl batted thick eyelashes and reiterated that her name was Kolina. And the baby, he was informed, was Lexandra.

The impossible names swam in his head, and were then pushed aside by more important tasks that needed to be dealt with.

"Okay," he said, pointing at the oldest girl, "You are not Saffron anymore. You are Number One. And you are Number Two…"

He went on quickly, numbering them largest to smallest, and he could see that rather than being indignant about the name changes, it was exactly what they needed. Someone of authority to relinquish the responsibility to. Having established himself as boss, he confidently gave his first order.

"Now, Number One, I have to go see to your grandmother, and I am placing you in charge here. That makes you second in command.''

Adding another number had been a mistake, because the child's brow furrowed. He hurried on. ''Number One, you are to make sure each of these children sits quietly on this couch while I go to your house and check on your grandmother. Nobody moves a muscle, right?''

He was already calculating. What were the chances his road was open? Slim. If he had to hike cross-country, he could probably be at the big house on the point in ten minutes, going flat out.

It pierced his awareness that Number One was not the least impressed with military protocol or her new title of second in command. In fact, she was frowning, her expression vaguely mutinous.

''No,'' she said with flat finality.

''No?'' Cole said, dumbfounded. Apparently the child had no idea that he outranked her and was not to be challenged. In fact, her cute little face screwed up, and she let loose a new wail that threatened to peel the paint off his ceiling. Fresh tears squirted out of her eyes at an alarming rate.

He felt himself tensing as four other faces screwed up in unison, but they held off making noise as their sister spoke.

''Mr. Herman, we're not staying here by ourselves,'' she told him. ''This house is spooky. I'm scared. I don't want to be in charge anymore. I want to go with you.''

He only briefly wrestled with his astonishment that this snippet of a child was refusing an order. Obviously the other kids were going to follow her cue, and he did not have the time—nor the patience—to cajole them into seeing things his way.

As much as it went against his nature, he surrendered

again. Twice in the space of a few minutes. He could only hope it wasn't an omen.

He hurriedly packed a knapsack with emergency supplies, and then he turned his attention back to the children.

For a man who could move a regiment in minutes, getting those five children back through the door, arranged in his SUV and safely belted into position was a humbling experience.

Precious moments lost, he finally fired up the engine. Just as he had feared, at the first switchback in his own driveway a huge ponderosa pine was lying lengthwise across it, the branches spanning it ditch to ditch. He'd reversed, plotting furiously the whole way.

The children spilled out of the vehicle and back into the house. He took the baby and lined the rest of them up, shortest to tallest, and inspected them. They were all dressed inadequately for even a short trek along the roughly wooded shores of the lake.

Biting back his impatience, Cole pulled sweaters and jackets off the hooks in his coat closet. "Put them on."

Giggling slightly, the children did as they were ordered. Cole stuffed Kolina inside a large sweater. It fit her like a sleeping bag. He intended to carry her, anyway.

He used pieces of binder twine to adjust the clothing on the older children so they wouldn't be tripping as they walked. Lastly, he looked for head coverings. Well versed in the dangers of hypothermia, he knew the greatest heat loss was from the head area. In a moment of pure inspiration, he raided his sock drawer and fitted each child with a makeshift woolen cap—one of his large socks pulled down tight over their ears.

He inspected them again. They looked like a ragtag

group of very adorable elves, but he had no time to appreciate his handiwork. Once more, the children were herded out the door.

He put the smaller of the boys on his shoulders, and then had Number One hand him Number Four, the toddler, Kolina, and Number Five, the baby.

He set as hard a pace as he was able, changing Number Three, on his shoulders, with Number Two, the bigger of the boys, every five or six minutes so that none of them would tire. The girl, Saffron, showed remarkable endurance. The beam of the flashlight picked out the well-worn trails that wove around the lake and to the point of land where the movie star's house was. To his intense relief the ax stayed in his pack. There were no obstacles so large that they could not get around them, though the path was littered with tree branches, cones and needles. Debris continued to rain around them as the wind shrieked through the trees.

It would have been a two minute drive to the house from his cabin. Overland, they made it in just over thirty minutes, which Cole thought was probably something of a miracle.

The children did not whine, or cry or complain. Soldiers could be trained to be brave. That the bravery of the children came to them so naturally put his heart at risk in ways it had never been risked before.

He heard the weak voice calling into the night before he saw her.

"Children? Where are you? Saffron? Darrance? Calypso? Kolina? Lexandra? Dear God, where are you?"

They cried back and began to run, and moments later were reunited with their grandmother. Their unbridled exuberance at finding her returned to life was nearly as exhausting as their sorrow had been.

Cole managed to herd the whole gang, including Granny, whom he secretly labeled Number Six, into the dark interior of the house.

The head injury had bled profusely. Granny's gray hair was matted with blood and it streaked her kindly wrinkled face and neck.

"This is Mr. Herman," Saffron told her. "We went to get him because we thought you were dead."

"My poor babies," Granny said, and then extended a frail hand. "Thank you so much for coming to my rescue, Mr. Herman."

He didn't really care if she called him Mr. Herman or Santa Claus. He wanted to assess her injury as soon as possible. The house, apparently electrically heated, was cold, and he herded his charges into what he knew must be called the great room. Located off the main hallway, it was a huge room with picture windows that faced the lake. In the dim light, he could see the floor was marble-tiled with thick Persian rugs tossed on it. Big mahogany-colored leather couches were grouped facing the window. Thankfully, on the north wall, was an enormous floor-to-ceiling stone fireplace.

He equipped the children with flashlights to help them find their way around the dark house, and then gave them each a job they could handle. The baby was set on the floor beside him while the rest of them went in search of clean cloth for bandages, ice and sturdy straight sticks suitable for splinting, should they be needed.

While they were gone, Cole opened his first-aid kit and began to swab away the worst of the blood. He grilled the old girl to see if she was confused, but, aside from being woozy, she seemed articulate and aware. She knew her age, the date, and even the impossible names of all those children.

She was not weak or numb on either side of her body, no blood or fluids were coming from her ears or her nose. She had not vomited or had convulsions that she was aware of.

Still, Cole knew the very fact she had lost consciousness made the injury serious. The roads were impassable and the phones were out.

But for him, handling emergencies on his own, without counting on backup, came as naturally as breathing.

The children brought him sheets, and, even the rough soldier that he was, he recognized them as very expensive. Percale. Unhesitatingly, he tore them into bandages and encouraged the children to do the same.

Children two, three and four were soon hauling wood. He settled Granny on the couch, built a fire, and, with Saffron at his side, began to haul mattresses down from upstairs.

''This is the boys' room,'' Saffron told him. The room was done in a jungle theme, complete with fake palm trees with stuffed gorillas swinging from them.

Saffron's own room paid homage to a vapid-looking girl who was too skinny and had too big a mouth. Brittany or Tiffany or something. The room was divided by an invisible line, and the other half—Kolina's, Saffron informed him—was aggressively Dalmatian. There were black-and-white spots everywhere. They marched relentlessly up the walls and across the ceiling, they dotted the rugs, the bed comforter, the pillows, the dresser and drawers.

Cole tried to decide which half of the room was more nauseating, but reached no conclusion. After salvaging both mattresses from the room, he closed the door firmly, hoping never to have to enter again.

The baby's room was a dream of ruffled white lace. It was everywhere—skirting the crib, forming a drape over it, hanging in big wads from the windows.

And those kids had thought his house was spooky!

Shaking his head, he began to haul mattresses down the curved marble staircase. It was easy to see why it had caused such a terrible injury. The marble was slippery and exceedingly hard. He shook his head at the impracticality of it.

In the great room, he laid out the mattresses and got his now-willing little soldiers to haul bedding. One last emergency before he tucked them in.

The baby needed fresh pants and badly.

"There's only a few diapers," Granny told him weakly. "The housekeeper will bring new ones with the grocery order tomorrow."

Cole didn't want to be the one to break it to her that the housekeeper probably wasn't coming tomorrow. He made a mental note to check around and see what was available that would pass as a diaper.

The diaper was absolutely rank. He had to tie the triangular bandage from his first-aid kit around his nose to even begin to deal with it.

The children shouted with laughter at his impromptu face mask and his clumsy efforts to handle the diaper. "This is a Code Brown," he informed them, trying not to gag. "The other is a Code Yellow."

"Poop, Code Brown," his second in command translated for him. "Pee-pee, Code Yellow."

The children squealed with laughter though he failed to see the humor. The replacement diaper was finally in

place, more or less, the baby had a bottle and the rest
of them were assigned beds. He tucked them in.

They took his refusal of their requests for stories,
snacks and teddy bears with fairly good grace, but insisted on good-night hugs and did not even notice his
awkwardness in performing this rare duty. Then they
laid down their heads and slept almost instantly.

Granny was soon sleeping, too, and he set his watch
alarm to check her pupils every two hours. Exhausted,
Cole stoked the fire, pulled the sleeping bag he had
brought from his knapsack and fell asleep on one of the
large leather couches.

He awoke to find the toddler sitting on his chest, her
face three inches from his, her eyes locked on his, willing him awake.

"Me Kolina," she announced as soon as he pried one
eye open.

"Number Four," he corrected her. "Go back to
sleep."

"Baby tinks," she informed him. "Code Bwon."

His own nose had already let him know that. And that
was how his day began, with a baby stinking and the
unsettling discovery that at this rate they had a two-hour
supply of diapers. And the pace didn't let up one little
bit, until Number Seven appeared, two full days into the
siege.

There was still no power and no phone. The main road
was not open. Cole would not, in good conscience, leave
an aging, injured grandmother alone to cope with these
challenges, never mind the five rambunctious children.

And now Number Seven had arrived. And it didn't
appear that she was a housekeeper with a nice, fresh
supply of diapers, either.

* * *

"What kind of nut has five kids?" The voice was gravel-edged and deep, and the man who regarded Brooke Callan from the doorway of her employer's house made her heart drop like an elevator rushing down a shaft.

The man was glorious and having spent the last five years in and around the film industry in Los Angeles as actress Shauna Carrier's personal assistant, Brooke was now something of an expert on glorious men.

And their black hearts.

To her discerning eye, this one looked more black-hearted than most of them. He stood at least six feet tall, handsome as a pirate captain. He had the faintly disheveled look of a man so certain of his charms he could be careless about his appearance.

His denim shirt was unbuttoned and untucked, and the white undershirt underneath molded perfect pecs, a wide powerful chest, a flat, washboard stomach. His jeans, worn through on both knees, were so soft with age and wear that they clung to the large muscles of sculpted thighs.

The man had dark whiskers roughing his perfectly planed cheeks and his clefted chin. His hair, black and curling wildly, had not been groomed, a fact that just underscored his faintly brutal untamed charm.

In startling contrast to the darkness of his hair and whiskers, and to the olive tone of his skin, were eyes as blue and startling as sapphires. There was a certain light of strong command in them that Brooke did not see in actors, though, not even when they were trying their hardest to look menacing.

The man before her gave off an air no actor could ever imitate. His eyes held the shadows of things not spoken about in polite circles, and something in the chis-

eled and forbidding lines of his face warned her this was
a man who had been on intimate terms with danger.

The look in those sapphire-blue eyes was impenetrable, guarded and assessing at the same time. The lines
around the firm curve of sinfully sensuous lips was stern
and unyielding. He did not look like a man who would
laugh easily or often.

The man exuded power and control.

Only one thing stopped the picture of menace, of almost overpowering male strength, from being complete.

Shauna's baby, Lexandra, was stuffed under one of
his arms like a football, her large padded rump and ruffled diaper cover pointed at Brooke. Chubby pink legs
churned the air happily.

Nestled in the crook of the other strong, masculine
arm was two-and-half-year-old Kolina, her head resting
trustingly against that broad chest, her thumb in her
mouth. The child's face was dirty, but other than that
she was a picture of contentment. She popped out her
thumb briefly and gave Brooke a radiant grin reminis-
cent of her famous mother's.

"Hawo, Addie Bwookie."

"Hello, sweetheart." Brooke tried to keep her voice
calm. Who was this menacing man? What was he doing
looking so at home in Shauna's house and so comfortable with Shauna's children when Shauna herself was in
California making a film?

Brooke knew if she had ever met him before she
would never have forgotten him. He was not an acquaintance of Shauna's. The other possibilities made her quail
in her shoes. Was he a criminal? A kidnapper? An ob-
sessive fan who had somehow found out about this secret hideaway?

How often had she tried to tell Shauna she needed

more staff? Full-time guards, not just the housekeeper
and nanny who came during the day to help her poor
mother. But Shauna had this thing about her children
being raised "normally," not surrounded by live-in
helpers and armed guards.

Realizing now was a poor time for I-told-you-so,
Brooke drew a deep breath, tried to swallow her fears
and gather authority. It felt like a futile effort given the
unflinching gaze that rested on her with such unsettling
intensity. She knew she looked a wreck, her clothing
rumpled, her shoe broken, her hair a hopeless damp
tangle after her nightmarish journey here.

Still, she had to conduct herself with dignity and courage. The safety of Shauna's children might depend upon
it.

"What are you doing in Shauna Carrier's house?" she
demanded.

"Who's Shauna Carrier?" he asked with only the
mildest of interest.

Brooke eyed him narrowly, trying to sniff out subter-
fuge. Surely every man in the Western world, and perhaps beyond, knew who Shauna was.

At least every man Brooke had the misfortune to date.
They knew and had no scruples about using the personal
assistant to try to get closer to Shauna.

The fact the actress had been happily married for the
last twelve years seemed to make no difference to the
myriad men who wanted to make her acquaintance.

But Brooke decided the man before her looked capable of many things—not all of them kind—but sub-
terfuge? Nothing in the stubborn strength of his features
suggested he would see any need for it.

"Shauna Carrier," Brooke explained. "She owns the

house you are ensconced in. She's the mother to those children you are holding.''

''Well, that answers my question about who would be nutty enough to have five children. She's a movie star, or something, right?''

''She's not a movie star. She's an actress.'' Of course, it was the wrong time entirely for a debate on semantics.

''Whatever.''

His lack of being impressed was completely unfeigned, but it seemed to Brooke this unexpected visitor to the estate was not being particularly forthcoming.

''Who are you?'' she demanded, sliding the zipper open on her purse as a first step toward getting at the Mace she kept secreted in her handbag.

For this whole long trek, she had been cursing Shauna for her overly active imagination when it came to her kids.

The phone, Shauna had reported to Brooke yesterday, almost in tears, was not working at Heartbreak Bay. Shauna was a devoted parent, and she spoke to her children every day when she had to be away.

The actress had fallen in love with the wild Kootenay region of Canada several years ago. She had purchased lakeside property and built a home there, declaring the remote location the perfect place to raise her family, away from life in L.A. and the prying of the press.

To Brooke, it seemed if Shauna was determined to have a retreat in the Canadian wilderness she had to factor in minor inconveniences like bears and mosquitoes and unreliable phone and power service. Even cell phones—essentials of modern communication—were inoperable in the area because the house stood in the shadow of mountains that soared to dizzying heights.

Yesterday, Brooke's calls on Shauna's behalf had determined the phones were out because of a severe windstorm.

Shauna had only been slightly mollified by the news that her difficulties in contacting her children were being caused by technical problems. She had that *feeling*.

Brooke heartily hated that *feeling,* which Shauna had also had about each of the men who had dated Brooke since Brooke had joined her employ. And, in each case, it had been entirely, heartbreakingly correct.

And so, Brooke had been dispatched to check on things in Canada. The trip was nightmarish, as always. The final indignity had been a huge tree across the highway just miles from Shauna's lakeside estate.

"Ma'am, we're going to be a while cleaning up this mess," a road-crew member had informed her helpfully. "You might want to think about getting a room in Creston and trying later in the week. Or if you're en route to Nelson, you can go the other way."

But she was not en route to Nelson, and she wasn't about to be thwarted at this stage of the journey. She hadn't succeeded as a personal assistant to someone as famous and temperamental as Shauna because she lacked determination.

So, here she was, her shoe broken, most of her nylons left behind on the branches of a fallen tree she had skirted, her gray silk suit smudged, rumpled and stained beyond repair, her hair falling in her eyes and sweat trickling down her neck from the final climb to Shauna's cliff-top mansion.

Facing a gorgeous and mysterious man who felt like an adversary. Of course, lately, she felt pretty adversarial toward all members of the male species, fickle swine that they were. And the better-looking they were, the more adversarial she felt. No excuses needed.

Brooke's exhausted mind tried to figure out if she disliked the man before her on principle, or if she sensed real danger. It did seem like a horrible possibility that Shauna's misgivings might be founded, once again. The facts: a notoriously handsome stranger with ice-blue eyes and the look of a warrior king was in Shauna's house and held two of her unsuspecting children captive in his powerful arms.

Brooke tried not to let the terrifying thoughts that were flitting through her mind show on her face. What if the fierce-featured man in front of her was holding Granny Molly and the children hostage? Even if he truly didn't know who Shauna was, the house announced to any who glimpsed it that the owner had a great deal of money, if not a whole lot of taste.

"Who are you?" she demanded again, her voice stronger as she slid her hand unobtrusively into her bag and searched around for her can of Mace.

"Who are *you?*" he returned, unforthcoming. His eyes narrowed and flickered to where her hand was imbedded in her purse and then back to her face. "We're expecting the housekeeper, which you obviously aren't."

We're expecting the housekeeper. As if he lived there!

"Addie Bwookie," Kolina informed him by way of introduction.

"I'm Brooke Callan," she said. "Shauna Carrier's personal assistant." She debated offering her hand, but she would have had to pull it out of her purse to do so, and she had almost found the Mace. Also, both of his hands seemed to be full.

And then, while debating what tone to take, she realized she was just too tired to be civil or cautious.

"I want to know what you are doing in Shauna's house. Where is Grandma Molly?"

She realized she should have summoned the energy for a more civil tone, because she did not like the look on his face, the tightening of his jaw or the squint in his eyes one little bit. She found the can of Mace and wrapped her fingers firmly around it.

In a blur of motion, he set Kolina on the ground and caught the wrist of the hand Brooke had inserted in her purse. His grip was not painful, but it was relentless.

"Let me go," she said and felt the first surge of true panic. This man was obviously much stronger than her. If he was holding the children and Granny, did she think he was going to come out and admit it?

Of course not! He would take her hostage, as well!

"You let go of whatever you have a hold of in there first," he said quietly, and the calm of his tone abated her panic slightly. Her fingers seemed to loosen their hold on the Mace of their own accord, and he let go of her wrist immediately.

"Now put your hand where I can see it."

The authority with which he spoke gave Brooke the very awful feeling he had done things like this before.

Though he had not for a moment looked tense, she saw that he relaxed subtly when she withdrew her hand from her purse and let it drop to her side.

Even after he had let go, she felt the imprint of his hand on her wrist and felt the leashed power of his grip and his personality. Kolina, on the other hand, was oblivious to his threat. From her new station on the floor, she had coiled her arms around his legs and was peeking out from behind his knee.

"Of all the nerve!" Brooke sputtered.

"What have you got in there, a gun?" He spat out a

word that was not at all appropriate in front of Kolina, then took a deep breath as though he was gathering patience. He seemed a little confused about who was the suspicious party here!

"It is none of your business what I have in my purse!" She resisted a temptation to rub her wrist.

"This is not exactly L.A.," he told her. "And guns and kids don't mix. I can't even believe you'd think of pulling one while I was holding two babies."

"Not a baby," Kolina informed him with a piqued pull on the leg of his jeans.

In spite of her indignation, Brooke registered the slim comfort that he actually seemed concerned about the children's welfare.

"How do you know where I'm from?" she demanded.

"You already told me you work for the movie star. We don't have a big film industry here in Creston, B.C. Besides, if the road crew is in the same place they were in yesterday, you've walked less than two miles and you look like you have survived a two-year trek across an unmapped wilderness. We make Canadian girls a little tougher than that."

His gaze moved to her torn panty hose, which fluttered in the wind, and she felt a strange but not completely unfamiliar twist in her tummy.

Her worst enemy, attraction to the opposite sex.

No wonder she was so determined to believe he was a villain!

So she could be glad that she looked terrible. More than glad. She should be deliriously happy. But, oh no, Brooke-who-dances-with-temptation was shattered by the appraisal of the cool stranger before her.

Insanely, even if he was a notorious criminal, she had

a purely feminine desire to be found irresistibly attractive by him.

Survival, she told herself. A little attraction might sway the power a bit in her direction if need be.

Besides, she liked basking briefly in male attention until they either found out who she worked for or Shauna appeared in person. Though reasonably attractive, Brooke could not compete with the stunning otherworldly beauty of her employer and had long since given up trying.

But this stranger seemed indifferent to Brooke's female allure even without Shauna's presence outshining the sun.

He continued his assessment of her in a flat tone. ''Your hair color is fake and your tan is real.''

''Canadian girls don't dye their hair?'' she asked sourly.

''They don't have that golden-girl look about them,'' he said. ''You do.''

He did not say it as if it were a compliment, and, unfortunately, when Brooke thought of golden girls she thought of Bette White and Bea Arthur.

''That's an awful lot to know about a person in a glance,'' she said, irritated at having been found superficial and inadequate without a fair trial. By a potential criminal.

And he wasn't finished with her yet!

He ignored the challenge in her statement and went on, his voice low and level. ''Don't ever touch a gun unless you are prepared to use it. And you know what? I can tell from looking at you, you don't have what it takes to use it.''

She stared at him in confusion. She should be delighting in the fact that an outlaw who had just taken over a house and kidnapped children would hardly be giving lessons on gun safety. On the other hand, he obviously had an unsettling personal knowledge of weapons and how to use them.

She felt a little finger of fury. How could he tell, in the length of a thirty-second meeting, whether or not she had what it takes? She itched to give him a little taste of the Mace.

"I do so have what it takes!" she said and realized it was a pathetic thing to say in the presence of a man who so obviously possessed the real thing in astounding abundance.

She wondered if she really could use Mace on him. She'd seen how quick his reflexes were. He could probably wrestle her weapon away from her before she'd figured out how to discharge the spray. And then, he'd be in the position to use it on her. She could feel the blood drain from her face at the thought.

"Exactly," he said and, looking directly into his piercing gaze, she had the disconcerting sensation that he had just read her mind.

For just a second, the briefest spark of humor flickered to life in the depths of those eyes. If anything, it only made him look more dangerous. And more attractive. And more sexy. She felt that traitorous little twitch of her heart.

She could almost see Shauna rolling her eyes and saying with sweet southern sarcasm, "Brooke, you sure know how to pick 'em."

"It isn't a gun, anyway," Brooke defended herself. "It's Mace. And Lexandra wouldn't have been hurt had I used it. I would have been very careful with my aim. Besides, there's quite a bit of padding between me and her skin."

"And for what reason exactly were you feeling a need to defend yourself?"

"I don't know who you are! Or what you are doing in my employer's home. With her children tucked under your arms. You haven't exactly been forthcoming."

"Ah. And straight from the embrace of Hollywood, you figured a plot was being hatched." His voice, edged with sarcasm, was even sexier than when it was not. "Let me guess, your boss is filming suspense and terror, and all of you become so immersed that you see it everywhere. An easy leap to assume I have taken the children and their dear granny hostage."

She disliked being so transparent, and, as a matter of fact, Shauna *was* filming a suspense thriller.

"Have you?" she said.

He snorted derisively. "Is it that easy to come up with a plot?"

"You are still not answering the question! You are being evasive, a quality I cannot stand in men."

The smile died. He looked at her intently before saying, with disconcerting softness, "I think I hear the bitterness of experience."

"No, you don't!" she lied, a defensive lie if she had ever told one.

He sighed, then dismissed that topic with a shake of his head. "It's the other way around," he said. "I haven't taken them hostage, they have taken me. I'm glad I don't do this for a living. It's exhausting being a hero. And then to get sprayed with Mace for my trouble."

A hero? No, no, no! "I would have used it only if you did something to deserve it."

"I don't believe that. Once you got your finger on

that sprayer, you would have been a dangerous woman. Trigger-happy.''

She did not dignify that with a reply.

''Mace is illegal in Canada,'' he informed her dryly. ''If they'd found it on you at the border you could have been refused entry. And that would have been a very bad thing for me, since I'm assuming you are the reinforcements, Addie Bwookie.''

''Brooke Callan,'' she corrected him haughtily.

But she registered the word *reinforcements* and her relief grew. Whoever the mystery man was, he wouldn't be glad to see her if he was up to no good, though *glad* was probably phrasing his reaction to her arrival a little too strongly.

Her relief died abruptly. What if he was that handsome, that sure of himself, that physically perfect, and he wasn't the bad guy?

He looked down suddenly at the baby that was straddled over his arm and a terrible expression crossed his face. He unraveled Kolina's fingers from around his knee, scooped her up, tucked her under the other arm, whirled and disappeared into the darkness of the house, giving Brooke little choice but to follow him.

Out of pure defiance, she stuck her hand back in the purse and fondled her Mace can deliberately.

Please be a bad guy. Please, please, please.

''Don't even think it,'' he warned her without looking back, and so she took her hand out again, not knowing what it was in his voice that made it unthinkable not to obey, but resenting it heartily all the same.

Chapter Two

Cole Standen's arm was drenched in baby pee, and the gorgeous, but irksome, Miss Brooke Callan was still toying with the idea of spraying him with Mace.

"Don't even think it," he told her and could feel her disgruntled shock that he knew exactly where her hand had gone the moment his back was turned. He'd spent his entire career assessing situations that involved matters of life and death, and he'd gotten damn good at reading people. She was still bristling with suspicion, and it had probably been a poor idea to turn his back on her, even though she looked as if she would weigh all of a hundred pounds soaking wet.

The fact that she had that poorly disguised look of a woman who was suspicious and prickly around all men only made her more dangerous.

But it was in reading his own reaction to the unexpected arrival of yet another complication in Heartbreak Bay that unsettled him. The truth was, Cole had felt a little shock of his own. Because the can of Mace in her purse was not where the danger from Brooke Callan lay. Nor was it in the prickly attitude he recognized as a disguise for fear.

Nope. It was from her eyes, huge and violet as pansies. There was vulnerability in those eyes. They were the eyes of a woman who had been hurt and was scared to death to be hurt ever again.

Thankfully, he knew the hard truth about himself: Cole Standen, least likely to be trusted with vulnerability. He wasn't going to hurt her. He wasn't going to allow himself to get close enough to hurt her. Nope, he was going to work overtime at keeping those defenses of hers—the ones that would have made a porcupine proud—in place.

No matter how attractive he found the rest of the package. And he did find it attractive, oddly even more so because of the broken shoe, the panty hose bunched around her shapely legs like the tattered remains of a storm-tattered sail, the wildly tangled brown hair, the rumpled clothes clinging to a delicate figure that was soft and round in all the right places.

Despite the smudged makeup and the defensive expression, her face was lovely, with high cheekbones, snub nose and wide, sensuous lips.

But quite frankly, everything about her was adding up to maiden in distress, and Cole Standen would have thought that after the last twenty hours, maidens in distress would have little appeal for him.

Make that two small maidens, one old granny, two lovable ruffian boys and a baby who was sweet and affable until the exact second Cole tried to set her down somewhere. Even if the adorable Number Five was sleeping, the moment he tried to divest himself of her, she shook herself from deep slumber and roared back to life. Number Five was setting up permanent housekeeping in the crook of his arm.

He'd retired from the rescuing business. He'd done his duty in some of the saddest, hardest, most shattered places in the world.

At thirty-eight, a major in the Canadian Armed Forces, he was burned out. He'd given his work and his career everything he had, up to and including his soul. He had no wife or children as other men his age did, and he was glad he didn't.

He did not think his job had made him a likable man. His emotions, by necessity, had turned to stone a long time ago. He had lived largely in the disciplined but rough arenas of all male societies. His areas of expertise included being able to strip and clean a weapon with astonishing rapidity, leaping out of aircraft without causing injury to himself or others and taking command of people in situations that tended to either bring out the best in them or the very, very worst.

None of these skills, so useful and lifesaving in his limited world, had any value at all when it came to the dreaded R word. As in relationships. With the opposite sex. Of the intimate variety.

Women, unfortunately, did not seem to get that. They threw temptation in his path by insisting on seeing him as a romantic figure instead of what he was.

Flawed. Cole knew he had come of age without a single skill that would make him a suitable partner to a member of the fairer sex, and especially not to one who looked as vulnerable as Brooke Callan.

He considered himself a natural-born leader who specialized in survival—and that meant the parts of him that were analytical and hard and cold and emotionally unavailable were overdeveloped. Way overdeveloped.

No, Major Cole Standen was exactly where he needed to be.

Alone.

After so many years of living a regimented, disciplined life, it was wonderful to wake up in the morning with nothing to do and nowhere to go, no crushing world disaster to feel in some way responsible for.

At thirty-eight, he had twenty years of service with the military and his pension was decent for a man of simple needs.

He had his boat, a cabin cruiser with a huge engine, moored at his pier, and for the past ten months, summer and winter, he'd fished the waters of Kootenay Lake. The body of water was as temperamental and hazardous as a mistress, and he enjoyed her changing face and challenges enough that he needed no other.

He'd been asked to write a book about some of his experiences, and, in the back of his mind, he thought eventually he might, but it never seemed to be a convenient time. And he didn't feel like pulling scabs from scars just beginning to heal over.

His life, until a little less than twenty hours ago, had been about as perfect as he could make it. No wars beckoned, and no one's life depended on him. So, he fished. He had a satellite-television dish. Occasionally he hiked the familiar boyhood trails of the mountain ranges behind his home. He kept a good stock of cold beverages, convenience foods, and T-bone steaks. He ate microwave popcorn for breakfast if he damn well pleased. He grew his hair so that it actually touched his collar at the back.

He was what every man longed for and every man envied. Cole Standen was free.

And then that little girl clutching a baby had come to

his door in the middle of the night. Even though he was an expert on handling disasters, his well-ordered world felt as if it had been tipped on its axis from the moment he had opened his door.

And now it tilted more wildly still. Brooke Callan appeared to be a new twist in the horrible unraveling of the retired major's perfect and controlled life.

Exposure to the genuine sweetness of Granny and those kids, with their incessant demands for hugs—never mind all their other constant demands for food, games, stories, clothing, snacks, noses wiped, bottoms wiped, diaper changes—seemed to be wearing him down, tenderizing the toughness of his heart, because why did he feel the threat of this woman so strongly?

And it had nothing to do with her Mace. Though he hoped he didn't have to wrestle it away from her. Her curves, under her somewhat sodden outfit, were delectable, and if it came to a hand-to-hand struggle, he might win control of the Mace but lose control of something much more vital.

It occurred to him that maybe he'd been doing the man-alone-on-the-mountain routine for a little too long.

He deliberately changed his focus, away from her, her curves and her vulnerability.

"Number One," he called, turning away from the door. "Number One! We have a Code Yellow."

He was rewarded instantly with the sound of many feet stampeding across the floor above his head, and, moments later, Saffron, dressed in a winter jacket against the cold in the house, appeared on the top of the curved stairway, a heap of towels clutched to her chest.

"Auntie Brooke," she shrieked and dropped the towels, flying down the stairs and flinging herself at Brooke.

"She's not really my aunt," she informed Cole, just as if he cared. "It's an honorary title."

"And one I enjoy immensely," Brooke said, and then asked in a suspicious undertone. "Are you okay, Saffron? Is everything okay here?"

"Of course I'm okay. Everything is fine, Auntie."

She was a beautiful woman to begin with, but when her face softened with relief and then lit from within as she returned that wholehearted hug, Cole had to turn abruptly away. This was precisely why he needed to keep Brooke Callan sour, defensive and irritated.

Unfortunately, he turned back just in time to see her expression of delight deepen as the boys tumbled down the stairs. They were unaccountably attached to the socks he had given them to wear on their heads and still had them on. And when Brooke smiled at that, her lips looked distinctly and temptingly kissable.

Discipline, Cole reminded himself.

"I'm fine now. But it was soooo awful," Saffron breathed, and Cole noticed, not for the first time, that the child had a precocious flair for drama. She probably took after her mother. "Granny fell down the stairs, and there was blood absolutely everywhere, and she didn't move. Not even a blink. Not even when I shook her. It was like shaking a rag doll."

Boy Number Two chipped in. "I slipped in the blood, and I thought her brains were on the stairs."

Cole couldn't help but notice that Ms. Callan turned a little pale, though he told himself it wasn't for her benefit that he cut off the tale-telling.

"Number Two," Cole interrupted sternly, before the whole episode could be reenacted, "we have a Code Yellow here."

"Code Yellow. Thank God," the boy said to Brooke. "I hate Code Brown."

"You and me both," Cole agreed under his breath.

"Darrance, you don't say thank God, like that, you say thank goodness."

That was much better. Brooke had a prissy and disapproving look on her face. Her lips had thinned into a downward line that a sane man would not think was the least bit kissable.

But a man who had spent too much time alone on the edge of a mountain-shadowed lake could still see the puffy sensuality of that bottom lip if he looked hard enough.

"Mr. Herman says thank God all the time. And also thank Ch—"

"Code Yellow," he reminded his troops sternly.

To his satisfaction, Saffron broke away from Brooke, raced up the stairs and gathered the towels that had fallen.

"The children are cursing. And why on earth are you calling them numbers?" Brooke asked, folding her arms over her chest and tapping her foot sternly.

This was much better. Much, much better. A less vulnerable-looking woman would have been very hard to imagine.

But out loud, he replied, calmly, ignoring the challenge in her voice because he knew that would irritate her more, "Where I come from, that wouldn't be considered cursing, Miss Brooke. Not even close."

"And where would that be? That you come from?" she asked snootily.

Hoping she would chalk it up to evasiveness, a quality she had already told him she disliked in men—and it seemed imperative that she dislike him—he chose to ig-

nore her. "Just between you and me, I have never heard
such strange and unpronounceable names in my life."
He gave Kolina, Number Four, who was still wearing
what looked to be a silk party dress, an absent pat on
her messy hair. "This one has a name like colon. Who
would do that to a kid?"

"You'll hurt her feelings," Brooke snapped at him in
an undertone.

The accusation caught him off guard, and he scanned
Kolina's face for any sign of hurt. The child gave him
her toothiest grin, her psyche apparently undamaged by
his dislike of her name.

"She was named after the heroine in her mother's
movie, *Sinking of the* Suzanne. Kolina is a beautiful
name," she assured the little girl, who didn't have a clue
what they were talking about.

Obviously, he was supposed to be impressed. He
wasn't. "Suzanne would have been a good name. Solid.
Sensible."

"That was the ship!"

"Better than a colon."

"Kolina is a Swedish variation of Katharine," she
informed him regally.

"Yeah, so what's wrong with the English version?"
he asked.

He found he enjoyed baiting Brooke. Keeping her dislike for him high was going to be more fun than he had
originally imagined. The new danger was that he rather
liked how she looked when she was annoyed. Her
cheeks were rosy as apples, her eyes flashed fire, and,
with the barest little shove on his part, she could probably be coaxed to stamp her foot.

"Katharine," he said, "there's a nice sensible name

that nobody would ever mistake for an interior body part. It could be shortened to Katie. I've always liked Katie.''

She stamped her foot.

He felt a smile trying to tickle his lips, but he ruthlessly bit it back.

''Obviously you are lacking in creativity,'' Brooke said. The humorless line of her own lips should have made him think of his grade seven teacher, Miss Hunt. But it didn't. In fact, her lips didn't look one ounce less kissable. Not one.

''Lacking in creativity,'' he agreed without an ounce of regret.

Saffron returned, and he noticed *she* was apparently unoffended that she had been labeled with a number. Probably hated her name, poor kid. He was willing to bet she got teased at school.

''Code Yellow is a diaper change,'' Saffron informed Brooke importantly and then added in a confidential whisper. ''Pee-pee. Code Brown is poo-poo. Only we don't have any diapers left because a tree fell down over the road to town. We're using towels.''

Brooke stared at the pure-white towels. ''These towels are from the House of Bryan,'' she gasped.

He folded his arms across his chest, gazed narrowly at her, daring her to go on. Of course she did.

''They're worth a fortune. Look, they're embossed. It's a special order. It takes months to get them. Years if you aren't Shauna Carrier.''

She pointed out the silky, heavy embroidery, white on white so it hardly showed up, anyway, as if this was a detail he was supposed to care about.

''Surely you could have found something else for diaper material,'' she sputtered.

''At great inconvenience to myself, I decided not to

let Granny bleed to death or to let five small children fend for themselves. My humblest apologies if my methods, and my diaper service, don't meet with your approval, Miss Callan.''

"Ms.,'' she corrected him absently, looking somewhat grieved that he had had the bad manners to point out to her that he had come to the rescue of her employer's family. She tried for a conciliatory tone, which failed miserably. "I'm sorry. I didn't want to give the impression I wasn't grateful for all you've done, but—''

"Good,'' he said, cutting her off quickly, since in his experience the word *but* almost always canceled out every word that had come before it. "I'm going to take a wild guess that you are going to love what we did with the sheets.''

"The sheets? You're not using House of Bryan sheets for diapers? They're Egyptian cotton. Seven-hundred-thread count.''

He couldn't believe this. She looked intelligent enough. Could she seriously be working herself into a lather over sheets? She was, and who was he to stop her? In fact, he egged her on just a little bit, for the pure fun of it.

"Nope, of course we're not using the sheets for diapers.'' He waited until the relief flitted through her eyes before he continued. "Not absorbent enough. We used the sheets for bandages. Ripped them into nice lengths.''

"Ripped them?''

"You know, since you disapprove so mightily, Number Seven, I think the perfect job for you would be looking after diapers. Feel free to find something more suitable than the embossed towels, by all means.''

A myriad of emotion danced through the astonishing depths of her eyes. It was so apparent that she hardly knew what to be indignant about first. It would probably be years before she could forgive him for all the offenses he'd committed—using towels for diapers, cutting up sheets, assigning her a number *and* diaper duty.

Yes, he'd racked up years' worth of transgressions in a very short time. Not that he planned on knowing her for years, but still he was very pleased with himself.

She would hate him at least until the power came back on. Then he would make his exit riding off into the sunset, his armor in place, like good heroes always did.

"Number Seven?" Brooke said, deciding on which transgression to deal with first. She pulled herself to her full height—which was not considerable and had the unfortunate result, at least from his standpoint, of pressing her curves right into the soggy material of her suit.

"Lucky number," he said, as if he hadn't even noticed her chagrin. The apple redness of her cheeks was spreading to her ears, which were small, and her neck, which was slender. Unfortunately both items of her anatomy appeared as kissable as her lips.

"You are not going to call me Number Seven. Nor are you going to boss me around. I'm in charge now."

That would have been a laugh, if she didn't look so serious. For the first time, he felt a little heat in his skin. "You?" he snorted. Her? Not damn likely. Not in *his* army. Anybody who would arm themselves with Mace in a household full of children was obviously not up to the task at hand and could not be trusted with the weighty stuff of keeping this little outfit happy and healthy until the power was turned back on.

It was time to establish the chain of command.

"I'm in charge," he said quietly. "You are lucky Number Seven."

"Don't even think of me and lucky in the same breath," she said, thoroughly riled.

She was aiming for his own vulnerable spots, and there was no way he was ever going to let her know it! He vowed he'd go to his grave before she ever knew he'd considered her lips—and her ears and her neck— kissable.

"The person in charge doesn't generally fraternize— let alone whatever you are thinking—with the diaper changer."

Her mouth opened and closed like a fish gasping out of water. "Fraternize? Are you joking?"

"No."

"You are in my employer's house! You are the outsider here!"

"And you are in charge of diapers."

"You arrogant son of a—"

"Uh-uh," he said. "You'll have the children cursing. Can't have that."

"I want you out of my employer's house!"

"Believe me, I'd be more than happy to leave."

"So, what's stopping you? There's the door."

"Before I go I have to be assured that you're qualified to take over here."

"Don't be absurd. I've been in charge of the children many times."

"With a VCR that worked and a fridge full of Popsicles, I bet."

"Your point, Number Eight?" she said scathingly.

"The children are the smallest part of this job right now."

"I'm not following you."

"Okay, see if you can follow this. Do you know how to start a fire?" he demanded.

She folded her arms over her chest. Her nipples had hardened. He hoped that didn't mean she enjoyed a good battle of wits.

"With matches?" she answered back sweetly.

"How about keeping a fire going?"

"Add wood?"

"Lots of things that aren't difficult on the silver screen are harder than they look when you attempt them in the real world."

"I see I can add patronizing to your résumé—I'll squeeze it in right after arrogant and right before knows it all."

"Being a smart aleck will certainly get the job done around here. For your information, stoking a fire so that it lasts overnight is an art form."

"Gee, I'll cash in my ticket to the Louvre so I can see that instead."

"Cooking over an open flame is also something of an art, too. Ever done it?"

"Of course."

"In the absence of hot dogs and marshmallows, that is?"

Silence, finally, but she was fuming. At least she was listening. Now he could start hitting her with the serious stuff.

"How about head wounds? Do you know how to watch for signs of concussion? Do you know a bad head injury, not monitored properly, can lead to death?"

He had her complete, if reluctant, attention now. "If Granny's wound starts bleeding again, do you know how to stop it?"

She was glaring at him. He'd hoped she'd stamp her foot again. She tossed her hair over her shoulder, which was nearly as good.

"Do you know how to dress a wound?" he said, pushing his advantage.

"I think I get the point."

But he was going to make damn sure she did. "Do you know what the temperatures can dip to in this part of the world at night at this time of year?"

Her silence told him he was nailing home his point, so he knew now was no time to ease up. "Do you know what hypothermia is, and how to treat it in the event you should let that fire go out?"

"Do you know how disagreeable you are?" she finally countered.

"As a matter of fact, I do know exactly how disagreeable I am. And you haven't seen the half of it. I'm saving that for when you cross me." Not *if* he realized, but *when*.

"I have rarely disliked a person as much as I dislike you."

Mission accomplished. "Gee, you're hurting my feelings. Now, take this baby and do your job, while I do mine."

He sniffed the air as he handed the baby over.

"Unless I'm mistaken, and I rarely am, Code Yellow just became Code Brown."

Saffron, completely in tune to where the balance of power lay, placed the towels in Brooke's free hand.

Brooke Callan was so angry she was shaking. She could feel her limbs trembling as she reached out to take the baby, and it wasn't because this house was so cold that the hypothermia he had talked about was probably imminent.

"Since you're in charge, your royal bossiness, why don't we have heat in here?" She should just let him have the last word, but she couldn't. It wasn't in her nature to be submissive.

"Electric heat," he told her. "No power, no heat. No lights, no refrigeration, no hot water, no oven, no microwave."

Though she wasn't going to admit it, maybe it wasn't such a bad thing he was in charge. No hot water? She desperately needed a shower. Desperately.

"Come with me."

Taking a solid hold of the baby, who indeed had an odor washing off her that heralded the crossing of the line between Code Yellow and Code Brown, Brooke followed him through the doors, which had been closed for the first time in her memory, into the main living room.

The opulent room had been turned into a refugee camp. In a glance, she saw the floor was covered with neatly made mattresses, the coffee table held piles of neatly folded rags that had once been the world's most expensive sheets. Cooking utensils and dishes were clean and piled neatly in front of the fireplace, where a fire burned brightly. Wood was stacked to one side.

The room was delightfully warm and smelled like barbecued food.

Granny Molly was stretched out on a mattress in front of the fire, her head swaddled in those very expensive bandages.

"Oh, Granny," Brooke said and rushed to her, the humiliations she had so recently suffered completely forgotten. Thank God he had been here!

"I'm fine, dear. It is good to see you, though." She lowered her voice. "I'm afraid Mr. Herman has been having a time of it by himself. Rather reminds me of that handsome Baron Von Trappe in *The Sound of Music*. He calls me Number Six. Isn't that adorable?"

Number Seven failed to see how.

"Do you think you could look after that Code Brown before we have to fumigate?" he asked.

"Are you certain you're all right?" she asked Granny, really concerned, of course, but also letting him know there would be no jumping by her to do his bidding.

"Oh, I'm such an old fool," Molly told her hoarsely. "Fell down the steps and banged my head. Poor Saffron thought I was dead."

"Stupidest steps I've ever seen," he interjected. "Marble. Slippery and hard. What kind of fool would put steps like that in a house with five children and someone elderly?"

"You must be nearly ready for your other nasty pill," Brooke said. "Your negative energy is beginning to flag a bit."

"Negative energy," he snorted. "Let's hang a few crystals and burn some incense."

Brooke shot him a glare, but Granny smiled tolerantly. "Just as I said. Adorable."

"Let's agree to differ," Brooke muttered. "Where do I change Lexandra's pants?"

"He has a station set up, right over there. And he's keeping water warm beside the fire. Just in case. You know. Code Brown."

Was everybody in this whole house giving in to his autocratic nonsense? Granny wasn't just giving in to it— she thought it was great!

"He's an angel," Granny decided happily.

"An angel?" Brooke repeated. She thought her labels were much more colorful, not to mention more accurate. Kidnapper. Brigand. Pirate. Tyrant. Arrogant something-that-you-didn't-say-in-front-of-children-or-grannies.

"What have you been doing with the, er, soiled towels?'' she asked with all the dignity she could muster as she brushed by him on the way to the change station.

''Burning them. Outside.''

''You're burning House of Bryan towels?''

''Lady, I sure as hell am not washing them. But, hey, that's your department now. Do what you want.''

What she wanted to do was march out of this house and not come back. But how could she do that? How could she abandon these children to him?

''He'd have you swearing like sailors by tomorrow,'' she told the baby at the change station, which was, not surprisingly, a well-thought-out area.

Safety pins, clean clothes, a bumper made of pillows set up around an end table that he'd sawed the legs off of. She was pretty sure the end table had been purchased at a little antique store in France the last time Shauna had been there. A bargain, Shauna had gushed. Authentic Louis the Fourteenth.

It occurred to Brooke that she was being terribly ungrateful. The truth was, she had not fully considered the wide range of skills she might need to take charge of a house with no electricity, five children and an injured person. And further, she did not have any of those skills.

She had never been a Girl Scout. She had only been camping once, and she had hated it. She had been cold and uncomfortable the entire time.

No, she was a city girl through and through. Her job was making appointments and juggling her employer's impossible schedule. It was handling Shauna's mountains of correspondence, fielding her phone calls, making her dinner reservations and weeding out who was allowed to see her and who was not.

It was a challenging job, with lots of perks and lots

of excitement. Brooke could count on an adrenaline buzz at least once a day.

But suddenly, all of her considerable skill seemed rather silly, in the face of this. The humiliating truth was that she did not even know how to survive without power, without electricity to turn on and off at her fingertips.

How did she get to be twenty-eight years old without having that particular skill, one that suddenly seemed essential?

She did not like this. How long had she been around that horrible man? Ten minutes? Twenty? And now she was going to question her life? And find it superficial?

Because of him?

Not!

She surrendered to using the towels, just this once. She was surprised to discover she found a smidgen of pleasure in it.

Oh, the headache these towels had cost her! Shauna had seen House of Bryan products for the first time at a dinner at Brad and Jennifer's. Naturally, she had to have the full line—towels, linens, everything they made.

Only House of Bryan was back ordered. Didn't she know the cotton came from Egypt? Trekked across the desert by camels, if you went by the cost. And she wanted embossed? White on white? The silk thread was imported, too. Very difficult to get right now. She might as well forget it. There was a three-year waiting list.

Brooke had begged and pleaded and placed phone calls and sent flowers. She had flaunted Shauna's name shamelessly.

The towels had finally come for the price of Oscar tickets, Bryan himself happily seated in the spot that should have been Brooke's!

Wouldn't that man over there roll his eyes with cynical pleasure if he knew the whole story behind his choice for diaper material? What kind of judgments would he make about the way she was spending the minutes of her life?

Angry that she had been put under enough pressure to be considering these matters herself, she scooped up the baby and held the soiled diaper at a careful arm's length.

The baby, now clean, was having no one but Mr. Insufferable himself, and so Brooke surrendered the baby to him, before Saffron led Brooke out to the burning barrel that had been set up at the back of the house.

Once it had been a pristine white Grecian concrete vase, but what the hell?

Brooke tossed the towel in.

Again, she felt a small and guilty happiness at throwing the damn thing out. She saw matches beside the vase and decided she would burn it, too. Not that she had anything to prove to him, but what would it hurt to show him that any fool could light a fire?

She soon found out there was a little more to lighting a fire than striking a match, after all. And disappointing discovery number two was that used diapers did not good fire material make.

"If you want to leave that," he called out the window, "I'll look after it in a bit. It might need a little shot of gas to get it going."

He'd been watching!

"If you tell me where the gas is—"

"Forget it. We'd have to cut up more precious sheets if you caught your hair on fire." And he shut the window just like that.

Fuming, she went back into the great room. He was

sitting on the couch with a bowl on his lap, skinning carrots, and he barely glanced up. Granny, propped up, was slicing potatoes and chatting with him as if he was one of her oldest and dearest friends.

The boys, Darrance and Calypso, were carefully wrapping the sliced potatoes and carrots in tinfoil and then setting them in a bed of coals that had been expertly isolated from the main fire. Saffron and Kolina were shredding lettuce into a big bowl.

It grated her unbearably that he had this situation so under control. No, not just under control. Everybody seemed so happy, to know their place exactly, to be so delighted to have his royal autocraticness in charge.

The only one who wasn't happy and delighted was her. She was the only one who did not fit, did not know her place. She felt like an outsider, an ugly feeling that she had been running from most of her life. How wonderful it had made her feel to get the job with Shauna—like an insider, finally. Of course, was she really?

Or was she just the assistant to the insider?

"Can you take over from me?" he asked her. "I'm going to run down to my place and grab some steaks. They'll be thawing, anyway."

For a hopeless moment she thought her momentary discomfort must have flashed across her face and that he was trying to help her feel she belonged. But no, that would have been giving him credit for some sensitivity.

"Where exactly is your place?"

"Just over there. You can see part of the roof from here. And you can see my beach. The one shaped like a half moon. I've got the only decent sand on the bay."

It came together for her. That's why the children were calling him Mr. Herman! He was the man Shauna called the Hermit Crab.

Shauna had given him the name last summer after she and husband, Milton, had gone for a halfhearted canoe around the small bay, tired, and decided to sun themselves in the sand, instead.

His sand as it had turned out.

He had kicked them off his beach as unceremoniously as if they were vagrants. It was posted, he had pointed out. He'd had the audacity to be completely uncharmed by Shauna. He'd been indifferent to her celebrity, when she had hauled it out. He didn't want trespassers on his beach, and he didn't care what their names were.

Unaccustomed to her fame and her considerable charm not getting her exactly what she wanted 24/7, Shauna had fumed over her treatment.

Which added an interesting new twist to this whole dilemma. Brooke had to wonder how her employer was going to like it that the Hermit Crab had taken over her house. Was she going to be grateful enough for the safety of her mother and children that she would overlook past differences and slights? Would she see reason and forgive her assistant for not getting rid of the man as soon as possible?

Unfortunately that was not the Shauna Brooke knew.

"Can I go with you?" Darrance asked Cole.

"Are you done wrapping the potatoes and gathering firewood?"

"Yessir!"

It was obvious to Brooke the big man yearned for a few minutes to himself. But it was payback time, and she was not going to rescue him from the hero-worship she saw dancing brightly in Darrance's eyes.

"Okay. Sure you can come."

Again, suspecting him of being capable of even the

slightest gestures of sensitivity would be a very dangerous thing.

When he went out of the room, it was as though the air went with him. His energy was so overpowering that the room seemed suddenly empty, devoid of anything lively or of interest. It was not a good way to be thinking of him.

Nor was it good to wander casually over to the window and watch him find his surefooted way along a path that wove deep into the forest. His grace was pantherlike, his absolute comfort with those rugged surroundings obvious in the long confidence of his stride.

He slowed, stopped, pointed something out to Darrance. She found herself wishing he was not the type of man who would stop to point something out to a young boy eager to learn.

"I just love him so," Granny Molly said.

"Who?" Brooke asked, startled.

"Why, Mr. Herman, of course."

"Oh, who don't you love?" Brooke said with far more annoyance than she intended. "I doubt if his name is Mr. Herman. He's the one Shauna calls the Hermit Crab."

"He is? Then we must call him his real name," Granny said, missing the point entirely.

"I don't even know his real name. And you know something else? I don't care to."

Granny looked at her, startled, and Brooke realized she might have been a touch too venomous. But then Granny Molly smiled, that wise-old-lady smile that Brooke didn't like one little bit.

"My, my," she said almost to herself. "Oh, my, oh my."

Brooke rolled her eyes and then looked back out the

window just in time to see him disappear into the embrace of the forest.

"Please let the power come back on," she said in a whisper. "Please."

Chapter Three

"All right, my dear, quit lollygagging," Granny Molly said with a little clap of her hands. "There's much to do, and only a short time to do it in."

Brooke turned reluctantly away from the window. "What needs to be done?" Here was her chance to prove her competence! "Should I add a log to the fire? Would you like a cup of tea? Would you like me to organize a game for the kids?"

Brooke only hoped proving her competence would have nothing to do with unraveling that bandage from around Grandma Molly's head. Or diapers. She'd had enough of diapers for a little while. Particularly Code Brown.

"Tea? Wood on the fire? Games for the children?" Granny made a *tsk-tsking* sound with her tongue against her teeth. "Give yourself a shake, my dear. You have been given the rarest of things, and you must seize the opportunity. *Carpe opportunis.*"

Brooke was pretty sure Granny did not speak Latin, but she was intrigued nonetheless.

"I seem to have missed something. What opportunity am I overlooking?" It occurred to her she had been over looking at that man leaving, but she could only hope Granny had not noticed her interest in him. It was strictly aesthetic, anyway, an appreciation of the male form, nothing more.

"You have been given a second chance to make a first impression! Go, quickly, change. Do something with your hair."

So Granny had noticed her too-avid interest! Brooke could feel heat moving up her cheeks at her transparency.

Granny continued, "Not to offend, dear—"

Of course, lines that began with not to offend were almost guaranteed of doing just that and Granny didn't disappoint.

"But you look like you've been spit out of the spin cycle of a commercial washing machine."

Brooke looked even worse than she imagined, then. "I did have to climb over a tree to get here," she reminded Granny.

"Oh! I am not questioning your heroic effort. I am sincerely grateful for your dedication to Shauna, and to me and the children. But, child, you simply do not want to be looking like *that* with a man like him in the vicinity. No, no, no."

It was true! Brooke did not want to look like something the washer had spit out. She could hear the no, no, no echoing in her own mind.

"But I left my suitcase in the car!" she said. Nothing could persuade her to go back across that tree and lug the suitcase here, especially since there wasn't anything in it striking enough to overshadow a terrible first impression, anyway.

"Your things wouldn't do, Brooke. You have a gift for the understated, which is exactly what we are not looking for. Now quickly, up to Shauna's room. Find something extraordinary to put on. Something that will completely turn that man's head."

Sanity tried to speak. "I don't want to turn his head."

But Brooke recognized she was lying to herself. What woman did not want to be seen as irresistibly attractive, particularly by a man so utterly confident in his own skin? The temptation was to make him weak with wanting, to become Delilah, the one with the ultimate power.

Naturally, she knew she should fight this impulse in herself, but her argument sounded weak when she voiced it. "I can't wear Shauna's clothes. She'd kill me."

"My dear, my daughter may be eccentric, and she is certainly difficult at times, but she is not mean-spirited. You're wet and cold and you have come to the rescue of her children, and her dear, sweet mother." She waved her hand, a fairy godmother with a wand, and declared, "You may wear anything you want out of her closet. Anything. And if Shauna has something to say about it, she can say it to me."

Since her mother was the only person Shauna was ever intimidated by, Brooke could take this as a go-into-the-closet-free card.

Without a backward glance, she bounded up the stairs and into Shauna's suite. It was an amazing room, done up like a scene out of *One Thousand and One Arabian Nights,* which Shauna had done a remake of in the early nineties, at the beginning of her career.

And in this room was Shauna's secret. For all that she loved male attention, she loved only one man. That man was her husband, Milton. Together for twelve years, their devotion to each other was enormous, almost embarrassingly passionate. They couldn't even bear to be separated when Shauna went on film shoots. Milton always went with her.

But the room was unapologetically erotic, and Brooke felt uncomfortably like a voyeur as she scurried past the enormous round bed, cocooned in filmy swathes of silk hanging from the ceiling. She hurried into the huge walk-in closet and slammed the door shut behind her.

First, she confronted her own image in the three-way mirror. Worse than she had thought, even with Granny's warning. Her suit was ruined, and damp enough to be clinging in all the wrong places. Her panty hose were shredded and hanging in tatters around her ankles. Her broken shoe gave her a distinctly lopsided look. Her hair was flattened to her head, and her makeup was smudged.

But for a girl looking for a makeover, she was in the closet out of a dream. She was surrounded by the whimsy and brilliance of almost every established and up-and-coming designer in the world. Versace. Klein. Armani. Michael Kors. Pamela Dennis.

There were slack suits, jeans, dresses and gowns to choose from. Every color of the rainbow was represented, and there were many different sizes to accommodate every stage of Shauna's many pregnancies.

Except for the cold, which was numbing, even more so once Brooke had stripped down to her underwear, this was the most fun she had allowed herself to have in a long time.

Oh, it wasn't that Brooke wasn't well dressed. She was. The suit lying on the floor at her feet was Chanel. But her clothes were not fun. No, they were well-cut classic suits in subdued colors that made her look very businesslike and professional, and did not in any way suggest competition with her flamboyant boss.

Now, Brooke explored her secret side. She tried on the black leather miniskirt and the sequined top that showed her belly button. She twirled in front of the mirror in the peach silk lounging outfit. It had belled sleeves and belled pant legs and a plunging cleavage. She put on the beaded Indian-cotton dress that flowed around her, whispering of womanly mystery.

The cut, the fabric, the attention to the smallest detail in these extremely well-made and extremely expensive clothes accentuated subtly, and sometimes not so subtly, everything that was best about a woman: her softness, her curves, her sensuality.

The last thing on any man's mind if he saw a woman floating down a curving staircase in any one of these creations would be asking her to do a diaper change.

Her secret side explored, Brooke rehung the more exotic of the outfits. She bid a reluctant goodbye to black leather, peach silk and beaded Indian cotton and began to take down some of the more conservative outfits.

Sexy, but competent, was the look she was aiming for.

In the end, she nearly decided on the suede pantsuit, butter yellow, soft as a butterfly kiss. Being a touch too small, it hugged her like a glove and tried to spring open around her chest. She solved that by putting a dainty silk camisole underneath it. The pants looked as if they had been molded on her.

It was understated, classy, sexy. It was just the outfit she needed to correct that first impression.

Then, maybe it was the cold, or the hopelessness of fixing her hair without warm water, but she came abruptly to her senses.

The idea was to get rid of him! How on earth was she going to do that in an outfit like this? As amusing as it would be to turn his head, to have him *begging* to change those dirty diapers for her, it just wasn't her style. She didn't want *that* man intrigued by her. She didn't want even a hint of a romance.

Since coming into the employ of Shauna, every single one of Brooke's romantic interests had ended precisely the same way. In disaster. There was no sense inviting disaster when it seemed to find her easily enough with no invitation.

With one last longing look at the temptation that flitted from every single one of those hangers, Brooke closed the door on Shauna's closet and went to Milton's.

Dear sweet Milton. His closet was no bigger than a broom room. Hanging there was a small collection of jeans, cords, T-shirts and sweatshirts, not a name brand among them.

Brooke took a pair of jeans randomly and slid them on. She rolled them up at the ankle and belted them at the waist. She tossed on the ugliest sweatshirt she could find. At least she was warm, she told herself, and dressed for duty. The outfit was perfect for executing diaper changes and roughing it without power.

She went into the bathroom, washed her face clean in the freezing water, damped down her hair and scraped it back into a severe ponytail. She snatched a pair of fashion glasses from a selection of them on a stand beside the mirror and gazed at the damage she had done.

On Shauna the glasses would have looked funky and fun. Perched on Brooke's nose they just looked frumpy.

This was her plan. Having let him know with the outfit that she was not interested in his male attention, she would get Mr. Herman, or whatever his real name was, to divulge each of his secrets to her. She was smart, if nothing else. Within hours, she would know how to start fires, and stoke them, and how to cook with no electricity. She shuddered at the thought, but yes, she was going to have to learn how to change those bandages, too.

And then she would dismiss him.

The pleasure of that moment would far outweigh any pleasure she would have gotten from watching his eyes widen with frank male appreciation when she first appeared in a black miniskirt and a top that showed her belly button. She hoped.

What would the point of playing dress-up be, anyway? To tempt him. To get him to play that man-woman game of shifting power and intrigue with her. But for what reason? She had already proved quite adequately that she was not good at that game. She had no interest in ending up with a bruised ego and hurt heart again when Shauna put him to the test.

Shauna's test. For all her flaws, Shauna was a wicked judge of character, a fact Brooke had found out, the hard way, shortly after she had joined Shauna's staff.

The man's name had been Keith. He had been extraordinarily handsome, supremely articulate and charming. Brooke fell hard. Shauna, more indoctrinated in the illusions of the world she moved in, had been cynical from the start. She had developed the test, which Keith had failed—with flying colors.

The object of the test, Shauna claimed, was to protect Brooke from men who would have no compunction about using her to gain influence with Shauna.

Though, naturally, Brooke was somewhat grateful to have scoundrels unmasked before she entwined her life too much with theirs, the unmasking hurt nonetheless.

Shauna's test had two parts, the first was called the flirt. Shauna, who had never been unfaithful to Milton, had perfected the art of flirting outrageously. Her air of sizzling sexuality kept her in the headlines and kept people flocking to her movies.

Keith had forgotten Brooke existed after the first flutter of Shauna's eyelashes.

There had been one or two other prospective beaux who had passed the flirt, which encouraged Shauna to move on to part two, the promise. In this test, she hinted that she would use her influence to gain favors—acting jobs, scripts read, technical positions—if the subject would leave her beloved assistant alone to do her job. Not surprisingly, Brooke had been left alone to do her job.

It had been a number of years now since Brooke had even had a date, unwilling as she was to subject herself to the test. She was thoroughly convinced she was a magnet for the black-hearted and superficial, though of course there was an overabundance of both types in the circles her employment led her into.

With past experiences hardening her heart, Brooke committed to her current plan. Get rid of Mr. Herman, the hermit crab. Sooner would be better. He was a little too intriguing, appearing to be the exact kind of rugged and masterful man one could really let themselves believe in. Not to mention so sexy he set her teeth on edge. Finding a pad and paper in the upstairs office so she could take notes on fire-starting, Brooke headed down the stairs.

The front door opened as she was halfway down. With one more wistful thought for the peach lounge outfit, she tilted her chin proudly and descended to the foyer.

* * *

Cole Standen had spent the better part of the hour that he had been away from the mansion contemplating the complication of Brooke Callan.

Oh, he talked to Darrance and pointed out things boys should know about the woods—which plants were edible and which could kill, the deer track on the path, the chatter of the squirrel up above them.

He selected steaks from his freezer, nearly totally thawed, anyway. Giving his fly-fishing kit to the kid to study, Cole disappeared into the bathroom, washed and shaved in cold water, splashed a little aftershave on and changed into a fresh shirt.

But Cole did all these things on automatic pilot. His mind worked relentlessly, focused exclusively on her. In a flash of insight, a master chess player zeroing in on the strategy of the opponent, Cole figured out what she was going to do, what her next move would be.

He chuckled out loud and congratulated himself on his own cleverness.

Since demanding power had not worked, Brooke Callan was now going to try to take charge in a more subtle way. She would use her feminine wiles against him, and he was willing to bet she dressed up pretty good. She was from a fast-lane world. He read the *Enquirer* headlines standing in line at the supermarket, just like everyone else. In her world, people used all forms of manipulation to get what they wanted.

This was his bet: he'd come back to the mansion on the hill and little Ms. Callan would have on her hunting clothes. She was going to be dressed to the nines, showing lots of leg and lots of cleavage. She'd have her hair done. She'd have on fresh war paint and sexy perfume.

His mouth got a little dry just contemplating the potency of an opponent of this caliber.

She was going to try very hard to wrap him around her feminine little finger. She was that kind of woman. She wanted the upper hand. And she wanted out of diaper duty.

Aware of what he was going to be up against, Cole spent the uphill hike back to the mansion preparing himself. He'd been trained to come through interrogation by the enemy—barring the use of truth drugs or torture—with his secrets intact, and the same methods could be used against Brooke Callan, femme fatale. He had a disciplined mind, and no matter how the outfit of her choice was designed to manipulate a man, to make him as pliable and soft as butter in her hands, he was focusing on other things.

Though he hoped to God she wouldn't be dressed in black leather. Or a miniskirt. Or God forbid, some combination of both.

He practiced a few scathing lines, like *Great outfit. Looks kidproof.* And *I hope you didn't squander any of our warm water on you hair.*

When he opened the door, he had firmly fixed in his mind a rifle in need of cleaning. No matter what she hit him with, that rifle was holding center stage of his mind.

Sure enough she was coming down the stairs. The rifle dissolved in his mind. It took everything he had not to bolt, and he didn't mean a rifle bolt either. Nothing had prepared him for an opponent of this much cunning, who could, apparently, thwart his strategies without half trying.

Coming down the stairs toward him was an unsettling combination of Tom Sawyer, with breasts, and a nun. Brooke Callan had horrible little glasses perched on the tip of her pert nose and a notepad stuffed under her arm.

He stared up at her, stunned. He tried to think of the rifle, but he couldn't. What game was she playing? And how had he, a genius at reading people, been so far off base?

"What is that you've got on?" he finally demanded, even though he ordered himself not to give her the satisfaction of commenting.

"Oh, I found some dry clothes to put on. I was freezing. You probably didn't notice my stuff was all wet."

Oh, yeah, pretty hard not to notice nipples pressing against sodden silk.

"Uh." Don't say anything else, he ordered himself. Not one more word. But that was his voice, defying orders, saying, "What? You raided the Goodwill box?"

"No, this stuff is Milton's. Shauna's husband. He's a pretty understated kind of guy."

No kidding. "Surely your boss has a better collection of clothing than her husband." Especially for purposes of manipulating and controlling the male of the species.

She shrugged. "Wrong style. Not me. You know."

Actually, he didn't know. In fact, he allowed himself to feel the insult of it. Women liked him. They wanted him to like them back. Some had gone to great lengths to get his attention, to win him over, to break down his defenses.

And Brooke Callan was dressed in a pair of jeans that would have fallen straight off her without the belt cinched up at her waist and a shapeless gray sweatshirt that looked like prison issue.

What was going on here?

He was a master strategist. How had this little slip of a thing managed to turn the tables on him? Well, they weren't staying turned for long. No, sir, as soon as he got those kids into bed tonight, he was coming up with a new plan.

He was going to kiss her!

He had no other motive, of course, than to see if she was as indifferent to him as that outfit suggested.

He knew all about how sneaky the enemy could be. She wasn't going to turn the tables on him that easily. He was going to turn them right back on her.

Besides, if her goal had been to achieve ugliness, she had failed. Frumpy, well, yes, in kind of a cute tomboy-ish way, but not ugly.

Her hair had been pulled back, sleek and shiny, into a ponytail. Worn like that, it showed off the classic line of her cheekbones and the grace of her neck.

And her eyes, unadorned with any makeup that he could see, looked unaccountably larger, the color deeper, so that they looked like the purple of a summer-night sky just before complete dark. Her lips were shiny, full, the color of peaches.

And soon enough he was going to know if they tasted as good as they looked!

The best defense was still an offense, he thought, as if he wasn't the least bit rattled by her outfit or his new plan. "Perfect choice of clothing. Kidproof. Suits you, too."

Hurt, before the defenses rose in her eyes. "I didn't have a whole lot of choice."

But he didn't believe her. He bet if he went and looked through those closets upstairs there would have been lots of things sexy and eye-catching, earth-stoppingly attractive.

"And thank you for not squandering the warm water on yourself. You're catching on to this emergency stuff with remarkable swiftness."

"Oh, you haven't seen anything yet," she said with such sweetness, he felt immediately suspicious. "How long does it take to heat the water? I mean, if I had used it on something as frivolous as washing my hair?''

Was it a loaded question? What was she saying that he wasn't hearing? Besides the fact that she had guessed he expected her to be frivolous, that was.

''You can boil it fairly quickly,'' he said carefully, ''to make soup or tea or to sterilize something. But then to use it for washing it takes nearly as long to cool, especially to a point where it won't burn the baby. So I keep some near the fire. It takes about two hours for two gallons to get lukewarm.''

She was writing furiously.

Trying to stroke his ego in another way? Make him feel big and important? He squinted suspiciously at her for a minute and realized it might work. He shook his head stubbornly and walked away. She walked behind him, scratching away furiously the whole time.

Now he knew it was true. She had a strategy of her own, and he was pretty sure it was to drive him crazy.

Granny looked up eagerly when they came in the door of the great room. Her eager look faltered and then turned into a frown.

''Good Lord, girl, have you lost your mind?''

''What?'' Brooke asked innocently. Granny snorted, and then turned her attention to a paperback romance she was reading. She deliberately held it up so she couldn't see Brooke anymore, apparently finding the younger woman's appearance nearly as offensive as he had.

Having been so thoroughly dismissed by Granny seemed not to bother Brooke even a little bit. She turned back to him, her pen poised. ''How many Code Browns a day? And how much water does that translate into?''

He shot her a sidelong glance. She had to be making

fun of him. But no, her expression was earnest, her pen ready.

"A dozen," he answered back.

"Lexandra is not doing Code Brown a dozen times a day," she said, but she said it uneasily. Unfortunately, that meant she didn't know any more about babies than he did. Not only had she shaken up his nicely ordered world, she wasn't going to be all that helpful to have around!

"I guess it just seems like that many," he conceded.

"How much warm water do we need?" she pressed.

"Diaper changes. A couple a day. And everybody washes, with soap before every meal or before meal preparation. So, I'd guess we're using five gallons of warm water a day."

"And the water works in all the taps? It did upstairs."

"Gravity fed," he informed her. She wrote that down, too, as if she had a clue what gravity fed was.

"I'll take the steaks outside and grill them." He'd only been back for five minutes and he already felt he needed to get away from her. She was unnerving in that he could not predict her behavior, nor see the motivation in it.

"So the barbecue works?" she asked, glancing up, looking at him over the rims of those detestable glasses.

"Propane," he informed her.

She wrote it down, then tucked her notebook inside the waistband of the too-large jeans. He caught a glimpse of her slender tummy. She could have fit a hippo inside those jeans with her.

"I'll just come out and see how you start the grill before I wash up the kids."

He shrugged and marched out the door.

The temperature was dropping, the wind was coming

off the lake and the automatic push-button start on the propane grill was touchy. He started the barbecue with a match, and then she insisted on trying it herself.

The grill started with a poof, and she leaped back from it. Some Tom Sawyer.

"Not bad," he said, "as long as you're not too attached to your eyebrows."

"Do I have any left?" she asked, her concern real enough for a woman who was determined to pass herself off as a scarecrow.

"Sure you do," he reassured her. "It's just that they're gray now and kind of curly on the edges. Next time, don't let the propane build for so long before you put in the match."

"It was the wind," she protested but followed her protest with more scribbling.

She scribbled and scribbled and scribbled. She scribbled during dinner and after. She wrote down how to make the potato packets in excruciating detail as if it was a recipe she was going to send in to *Gourmet*. She noted everyone's after-dinner jobs. She took careful notes as he changed Granny's bandages and prepared more for tomorrow. She watched as he stoked the fire for the night, writing step-by-step instructions.

Then she helped get the children into their pajamas and tucked into their beds. It was the first time she had put the notebook down.

The room was dark now, save for the flickering of the firelight, and despite the outfit and the glasses she looked very, very beautiful, snuggling with those kids. Her hair was falling down, she had a smudge on one cheek, and the sweatshirt was sporting little spots where the steak had spit grease on it. And she still looked beautiful.

"Mr. Herman, tell us a story now," Saffron requested with a yawn.

"Not tonight." He had other plans for tonight. Big, big plans. He glanced over at his quarry.

"Please, please, please." The chorus was deafening.

Brooke held up her hand. "First, before the story, I think we should find out Mr. Herman's real name."

"What is it?" they all called in unison.

"If you guess," he said, "I'll tell you. I'll give you hints, too."

This surprised him about himself. He liked the kids. He enjoyed playing these little games with them. He liked their energy, and their eagerness to learn. He loved the sense of adventure in their hearts that made an emergency like this one into a game. He liked how flexible they were about life, their willingness to laugh.

"My name is the same as something really black," he said.

"Like Mr. Night?" Calypso asked, catching on right away.

"Nope. Blacker."

"Black heart?" Brooke guessed, and again he caught a glimpse of her that was not sophisticated, but afraid. Afraid of men. For the first time, his commitment to his plan faltered. Had he forgotten the vulnerability he had seen in her eyes? It occurred to him that he had known from the start that was not something he should be playing with.

He handed out another clue. "They mine for it."

"Mr. Gold," Kolina decided.

"It's black, dummy," Darrance told her.

"Don't call your sister a dummy," he said sternly, "or Santa might leave you this, instead of a present."

"A lump of coal," Saffron cried triumphantly. "Your name is Mr. Coal."

"Actually Cole is my first name. My last name is Standen."

There was great fervor while they tried to sort out who had thought he was Mr. Herman and why.

"Isn't that the most suiting name?" Granny said.

"I'll say," Brooke muttered.

"Coal," Granny mused, shooting Brooke a look he couldn't quite interpret. "That's where you find diamonds, when you're mining for coal."

His plan faltered yet again. How could he steal a kiss from Brooke, when Granny thought so highly of him? Thought there were diamonds in the coal? Geez.

"Mr. Standen." The kids tried the name out one by one.

"Actually, it's Major," he said.

There was a brief awed silence. "Major Standen," Calypso said, sat up in bed, saluted and said, "Aye, aye, sir." The kids collapsed in giggles.

"I think that might be the navy," he said, but he was laughing, too. The room felt so cozy, warm, a sanctuary from the world where he had lived so much of his life.

"Now tell us a story," Saffron said. "About you."

He didn't think very many of his stories were appropriate for children. But he cast around in his mind and remembered one from his childhood.

"A long, long time ago there was a boy named Jimmy," he said. "He lived on the other side of the lake, straight across from this bay with his dad, who was a trapper. The only way to get over there, to this day, is by boat. Jimmy and his dad were isolated from other people. They only went into town a few times a year. Jimmy didn't even go to school. He was very lonely, but he had a gift with wild animals. He had a raccoon that was like a dog. It followed him everywhere and even rode in his canoe with him.''

He could see the raccoon had the kids completely captivated, but he was more surprised to see the look of intent interest on Brooke's face. She came from a place where stories were slick and told with many special effects, yet, in the firelight, her face reflected the same delighted interest as the children.

"Jimmy grew to be a man. He worked hard and lived off the land. He looked rough, but his heart was so gentle that when he sat on the beach the deer would come up to him and lay their heads on his lap.''

The children's eyes grew round, and Brooke sighed. So, she liked the gentle type. Oh, well.

"One day Jimmy looked across the lake to this bay, and he saw a house was being built. Often he would go visit the men building the house. They said it would be a summer home for a wealthy family that owned a mine.

"And one summer day, he paddled over and saw a girl walking the beach. He had not seen very many girls, but even so he knew she was beautiful. She had on a long white dress and carried a parasol, and even from a great distance he could see she was the most wondrous being he had ever laid eyes on.''

Brooke was leaning toward him, her chin cupped in her hands, her eyes starry. A romantic, then. He realized, not happily, he might have to revise his plan for this evening.

Her outfit had made him forget how vulnerable she was. His unfortunate choice of a story was reminding him of that.

"Jimmy landed the canoe and got out, and the girl stopped and stared at him. Remember, she had probably never seen anything like Jimmy before. He would have been dressed all in homemade leather clothing, buckskins. His hair would have been long, brushing his shoulders. He would have had that wild way about him of a man who has never been tamed.''

''I just love Jimmy,'' Saffron said, and for a frightening moment, he saw the handful she planned to be as a teenager.

Brooke must have seen it too, because she looked across Saffron's head at him and smiled with understanding.

Cole decided he had chosen a very stupid story to tell to females.

''She looked like she was going to run away, but remember, this was a young man who could charm deer from the bushes. He knew exactly how to handle frightened things.

''He turned and called his raccoon, and it came scurrying out of the canoe. Jimmy got down on his knee, and the raccoon ran up his arm and perched on his shoulder.

''The girl laughed out loud. And then he rose, and, never taking his eyes off her, he called a wild bird from its nest. It landed on his arm, and, very softly, he walked toward her and put it on her shoulder. 'I'm Jim,' he said.

''And she told him she was Eileen, and her love for him was already shining in her eyes.''

It was too late to turn back, but what on earth had possessed him to tell this story? Brooke was looking away, gazing at the fire, but he wondered, suddenly, what it would be like to see her eyes on his face with *that* look in them.

It was insanity. The fire and the quiet breathing of the children and the story were wrapping him in a spell.

"From then on she loved him. They would meet and explore his world, a world full of creatures and beauty beyond what she had ever imagined. He showed her the way he saw that world, with simplicity and reverence, and the world became something more alive and vibrant than she had known it could be."

He tried to hurry the story, but it was taking on a life of its own and would not be hurried. It was a classic rich girl, poor boy story. When her parents found out about Jimmy, they disapproved mightily. Jimmy's own father thought he didn't know his place.

"So, they decided to run away and get married. They agreed to meet on the full moon at that point right there."

The children all sat up in bed and craned their heads to see the point. Brooke actually got up and looked out the window at the lonely piece of rock that jutted into the bay. She shivered and hugged herself.

"But her father caught Eileen leaving that night, and he locked her in her room. So, when Jimmy came, she wasn't there, and he thought she'd changed her mind.

"A storm was brewing on the lake. Everyone knows you can't be out in a small boat on that lake during a storm, but apparently Jimmy did go back on the lake that night." He paused. Should he make up a different ending? Too late now, he realized. The truth had a way of sounding authentic, and he could not dishonor his ancestors by changing the story now, even though he felt a strange desire to protect Brooke from the ending.

She must have known, for she had not moved from the window, and she did not turn and look at him.

"They found his canoe broken on the rocks of her

beach the next morning. His beloved raccoon was alive, beside it. Nobody ever saw Jimmy again.''

Out of the corner of his eye, he saw Brooke heave a big sigh, swipe hastily at her cheek. How had this woman survived the shark-eat-shark world she had chosen for herself?

With a mask, he realized. A mask that made her seem cold and efficient and as if all she wanted was to be in charge.

He gave up his plan to steal a kiss. The idea had been to unmask her, but the story had done it just the same.

''Oh, that is so sad,'' Saffron said. ''What happened to the raccoon?''

''Eileen learned to call birds from the wild and that raccoon became her best friend. Despite the fact she was considered eccentric, her parents managed to marry her off to a man they approved of. Did he love her? The story says no. That he was ambitious and wanted a partnership in the mine.''

''People are like that sometimes,'' Saffron said wisely. ''I know because my mommy's famous and sometimes people only like me because of that.''

He saw Brooke tense. So everyone close to the great actress had to keep their guard up against being used.

''So what happened to Eileen?'' Brooke asked, reluctant to be as interested as she was. Her back was still carefully turned to them.

''She spent a great deal of time at the lake house. She had children, six of them. From all reports, she was a good mother. Gentle and kind and attentive. But one night, after all her children had left home, when the moon was full and a storm was brewing, she went and walked by the water. The next day someone found her white dress and her parasol on the very beach where that shattered canoe had been found. No one ever saw her again, either.''

''That is so romantic,'' Saffron said dreamily. ''Just like Romeo and Juliet. Well, sort of.''

''Is this true?'' Brooke asked sadly and turned to look at him.

He could erase the softness from her eyes in a second by saying he'd made it all up. But he didn't.

''That's why it's called Heartbreak Bay. Eileen was my great-grandmother. The Standens owned everything around here until mining went sour in the sixties. We kept the piece of land my cabin is on. Everything else was sold.''

''I like ghost stories,'' Calypso said, obviously disappointed.

''You'll like the ending then. There are people who say they have seen them, Jim and Eileen, walking hand in hand on moonlit nights on that beach. They say she's in a white dress and carries a parasol and that he's in buckskins and a raccoon waddles along behind them.''

''Ghosts?'' Saffron asked with a delighted shiver. ''Right here?''

''Good ghosts,'' he said, seeing that this might not have been the best ending to tell to such a highly impressionable audience.

''I like stories about bunnies,'' Kolina told him, as disapproving as Calypso. ''Mommy Bunny, Daddy Bunny, Baby Bunny.''

''I'll keep that in mind for next time,'' he promised.

''I like army stories,'' Darrance said. He got up on his knees, held up an imaginary machine gun and mowed down his brothers and sisters.

''I don't tell those kind of stories,'' Cole said firmly.

"Everybody, hunker down in bed. To sleep and that's an order."

There was a chorus of aye-aye sirs.

In the deep silence that followed, Granny sighed. "Well, I'm partial to a good love story, and I have a feeling, Cole, that your great-grandmother may still be looking for her happy ending."

"What do you mean?" he asked.

But she shrugged and tucked down deep in her mattress and closed her eyes.

He met Brooke's eyes over the old woman's head. He looked away first.

Chapter Four

Brooke lay awake for a long, long time, too aware of all the small disturbances around her. She was accustomed to big noises outside her Santa Monica bedroom—cars, airplanes, sirens, doors slamming, people chatting on the walkway outside her apartment.

Tonight, camped sleepover style on the living-room floor of Shauna's house, it was the noises inside the room that seemed amplified and disorienting. The fire flickered and crackled and occasionally popped loudly. Saffron sighed in her sleep and tossed restlessly. The baby cooed. Calypso wasn't asleep. Brooke could see him outlined by the fire, playing with some little toy he had brought to bed with him.

She was sure Granny, who had been sending her the evil eye every time she was within range, was tsk-tsking in her dreams. Granny's disapproval of Brooke had deepened when she had told her in a low voice, as they were getting the children ready for bed, to "at least find something decent to wear to bed."

Brooke had interpreted decent as a sacklike flannel nightgown she had found folded neatly in a basket of clean clothing in the upstairs laundry room. It was off-white, the print on it was large sunflowers.

"Is this yours?" she'd asked Granny, coming back into the room.

"I would never wear something so utterly nauseating," Granny had said. "It would probably give me nightmares. From the size of it, I'm guessing it was left behind by that comedian who visited in the fall. Don't wear it, Brooke. You'll frighten the children."

But the children had been sleeping by the time she had put it on, except for Calypso, but he didn't glance up from his toy when she tiptoed back into the room and picked her way over the sleeping children. Cole, stretched out on the couch, reading by flashlight, seemingly completely comfortable in these barrack-like surroundings, had glanced briefly her way, done a double take, and then looked as if he was nursing a very bad headache.

He had shut off the flashlight and left the room, giving her ample time to make up the mattress they had dragged down the steps for her, and go to sleep, but of course she had not. She had waited for him to come back, and he did not disappoint.

When he came back into the living room, Cole was bare-chested, a towel slung casually around his neck. His hair was damp and curling, suggesting he had actually stuck his head under the ice-cold water in one of the bathrooms. For pajamas he wore a pair of shapeless running shorts, in navy-blue sweatpants material, held up with a string at the waist. She wasn't sure why he did the baggy look such justice when she so obviously did not.

He looked utterly magnificent, his bare legs long and hard and strong, his chest and arms banded with taut muscle. His shoulders were wide, and his stomach was flat. He looked every inch the warrior that he was, and the firelight deepened his natural skin tones, making him look as if he were cast in bronze.

Granny, who at that time had still been awake, gave an unstifled moan of pure feminine appreciation that Brooke could only hope Cole would not attribute to her.

He cast a quick glance their way and raised an eyebrow. Granny, traitor, pretended she was sleeping. Brooke clamped her eyes shut, too, but opened them in time to see him slide into his sleeping bag, fold his arms under his head and close his eyes. His breathing became slow and steady.

Though not sure why, Brooke did not think he was sleeping either.

Her own mattress was on the far side of the children. Cole slept on the couch. She was as far away from him physically as she could get, but it was not far enough.

One by one, everyone went to sleep, even Granny and Calypso, but over all the other little noises and distractions, what she heard most was him, Major Cole Standen, his breathing strong and sure.

She realized she felt utterly safe in this room. Protected from all the catastrophes that waited in the dark corners of this house with no power, in those forbidding and mysterious woods right outside.

He was a man who would instill that feeling in people: things might go wrong, but not on his watch. At least, she felt physically safe, as if Cole would deflect any danger that came their way with easy confidence.

He had the air of a man who had tested his capabilities

many times and in many different conditions, and who had won.

But for all that Brooke felt physically safe, her heart was a different matter. By tilting her head just a little, she could see his outline on the couch, the depth of his chest as it rose and fell, the firelight softening the cast of his stern features, even the hard line around his mouth looked gentler.

It was very easy to think dangerous thoughts—what would those lips taste like? What would those immensely strong arms feel like wrapped around her?

She shuddered and shook off the thoughts, ordered herself to close her eyes. But when she did, the story he had told earlier insisted on haunting her, and not because of the two ghosts who put in an appearance at the end. It haunted her because of what it told her of him. He was not all strength and gruffness. She had caught glimpses of a gentle side when he dealt with the children.

But when he had told that story, something in her threatened to melt, just as if he had called a wild bird from a tree and set it on her shoulder.

Cole was like that young man in the story. There was something in him that was wild, somehow, untamed. He was resilient, completely at home in a world that required rugged strength and toughness. And he was very alone in that world.

And was she like the girl? Like Eileen? Cosmopolitan, from a different world, ultimately lonely for something only that boy could give her?

What had Eileen, a rich girl in a white dress and a parasol, seen in Jimmy, a barely civilized young man, with long hair, dressed in buckskin, a raccoon trailing his every step?

But Brooke, lying there awake, knew exactly what that long-ago woman had seen in that long-ago young man. Jimmy had been real. And all creation—even the birds and the animals—knew he was real. No wonder Eileen had remained unhappy long after he had died. After knowing someone so real, so genuine, so much without artifice, how could she have ever settled for anything less? For a world where people, like the husband she had been bartered to, sold their souls for material gain?

Something real. It was a quest Brooke felt almost irresistibly attracted to. But wasn't L.A., the film scene, Shauna's world absolutely the wrong place to search for reality?

When Brooke had begun her journey to these hinterlands, a little under twenty-four hours ago, this was not what she had expected. To get dropped into circumstances that were going to make her yearn for things she did not have, make her look cynically at her own choices, make her study her own soul.

She didn't even know how much of that bedtime story was true, and how much was romanticized nonsense. Not that Cole seemed capable of weaving romanticized nonsense on his own accord, he was just repeating family legend.

Still, somehow, it was all his fault that she could not sleep and that she was looking at the layers of her own life with dissatisfaction.

Because of his competence with handling whatever the world threw at him. Because of the way he had told that story, some yearning of his own in his voice.

She plumped her pillow, then turned her back on the fire and on him. She was just worn out from all the different challenges and experiences she had encountered. She was not thinking straight. Exhaustion had made her vulnerable to wayward thoughts.

She vowed, right then, she was not realigning her whole life because she had met a man—she had tried that before—and certainly not because she had heard a strangely compelling story.

No, she was sticking with plan A.

Tomorrow, he was going. Major Cole Standen was being given his walking papers, by her. Surely the electricity would be back on soon, the road reopened.

But the big thing was he had to go. She felt, physically, safer than she had ever felt, and, emotionally, more in danger. When he went, she was willing to wager this strange restless yearning inside her would go, too.

Finally, with her plan reaffirmed, she slept, but restlessly, her dreams held captive by a beautiful young woman walking a beach, calling the birds from the trees, a raccoon scooting along at her heels, and a shadowy man in buckskin watching her.

Cole was up early, nauseatingly cheerful, whistling a tune between his teeth as he got the fire going. Apparently he had no intention of putting a shirt on just yet. Brooke pulled a pillow over her head.

The kids did not wake slowly, either. They burst to life. In seconds, the room went from the silence of sleep to pillows flying, the boys wrestling, the baby screaming. Granny greeted the day with enthusiasm, as well, humming something from the *Lion King*. The words came to Brooke unbidden. Can you feel the love?

If Brooke was not careful, she might feel the love and happiness leaping in the room like a life force. But if she allowed herself to feel it, she might surrender to it and might want nothing to change, ever. A person could become addicted to mornings like this.

But of course her mission was to change things, though that mission seemed to waver as she allowed herself to be rousted from bed by children who attacked her with pillows, and it wavered even more as she helped prepare breakfast. She felt the sharp pang of regret. For a road not chosen, for the fact that somewhere along the line she had not met the right man and so did not have a happy houseful of children of her own.

The regret deepened as she worked side by side with Cole, and she realized they could be quite the team, if she allowed it.

"Like this," he demonstrated, breaking an egg into a bowl with one hand.

Scowling with furious concentration, she mimicked what he had done. The egg splintered, leaving her hand oozing yolk and white and sending shell into the bowl.

The kids howled with pleasure, and her dismay quickly melted. Brooke laughed. She glanced over to see him grinning.

The grin made him devilishly handsome. His teeth were straight and white, and his blue eyes sparkled like sunlight on a lake. Yes, he had to go.

But first, all the kids had to try one-handed egg breaking, an egg apiece. There was finally more shell in the bowl than egg, and Cole assigned Kolina to pick out the shells, a job she delighted in.

Finally, covered in egg and flour, the laughter still tingling in the air around them, this group of people who felt just like family gathered around the fire. Cross-legged and in their pajamas, they ate a feast of bacon, scrambled eggs and biscuits.

Despite the challenges of cooking, the food was done

to perfection. And despite her vow to cling to her typical morning grouchiness, Brooke could not resist the gleeful spirit, the happy bantering or the rich contentment in the room.

She watched as the kids fought to be near Cole, arguing over who got to sit next to him and flipping coins to see who would get the after-breakfast chores that would put them in closest proximity to their rescuer. The kids adored Cole, absolutely and without reservation.

And he, in turn, was a natural with the children, effortlessly hitting exactly the right balance between firmness and friendliness.

Brooke allowed breakfast, and all the chores surrounding it, to be out of the way before she dismissed him. Appreciating him would only make her job harder.

"Cole, I need to talk to you. Alone." She couldn't quite look him in the eye.

He followed her out into the hallway, and they stood at the bottom of the curved staircase that had set all these events in motion.

She took a deep breath, looked him in the face then looked quickly away. "Major Standen, I can't thank you enough for all you've done here."

"A minute ago it was Cole, now it's Major Standen. The last time the hair rose on the back of my neck like this I had the enemy creeping into my camp with knives between their teeth and treachery on their minds."

She wanted to hear that story. Badly. She wanted to hear all about his adventures. About his family. About his boyhood on this lake.

Treachery came in all kinds of shapes and sizes, apparently. How could she have known her own heart would have such a treacherous streak?

She pushed on with her rehearsed speech. "I know

Shauna will want to reward you in some way. Is there anything in particular you might like?''

''I actually find that insulting.'' He folded his arms over his chest. His forearms rippled enticingly.

Oh, God! Forearms like that, and he might be the one man Shauna could not buy. How unfair was that?

''I'll tell Shauna that,'' Brooke said, though she doubted it would do any good. Shauna liked grand gestures. Whether he wanted it or not, Cole was probably going to find himself in possession of a 46-inch flat-screen TV or something comparable.

It didn't make her feel any better about what she was about to do that he was determined to be an honorable man and that he might be able to pass the Shauna test.

Such thoughts only made everything feel worse— more tempting, more confusing, as if her well-ordered life was being sucked into a whirlwind.

''I've got all my notes,'' she rushed on, determined to stick with her plan. She waved them under his nose to prove it. ''So there really is no reason for you to stay. I'm sure you have your own life to get back to. I can manage here now.''

She snuck a peek at him.

He looked as if he was going to laugh at her proclamation of competence! So much for the peace between them!

''Are you dismissing me?'' he asked, his voice deep and sure. His voice was very sexy. All the more reason for the dismissal.

''Exactly!'' she said.

He looked at her long and hard. The laughter faded from around the corners of his mouth. ''Okay,'' he said solemnly. ''That's fine.''

She had expected a tiny bit of a fight. Oh! How hateful

he was! He wanted to get away just as much as she wanted him gone.

"I mean I know," she said, "that you've probably got many years of real-life experience with this roughing-it stuff and I only have a few notes and a few hours of knowledge, but I really think I can handle it."

"Great. You've convinced me."

But she could tell she hadn't. He thought she'd come running back to him within hours, begging for his help. She'd follow his great-granny into the lake before she ever begged Cole Standen for anything!

"The power will probably be back on at any minute," she said, feeling compelled to go on convincing him, even though he had already said he was leaving.

"Uh-huh."

"Well, what is the longest it's been out?"

"Three weeks."

"Oh. That's quite a long time." She knew she must not waver now. Three weeks was the worst-case scenario. "But it won't be that long. I just know it."

He did not look impressed with her deduction process, but he offered no advice, no argument about staying.

"Besides, the road should be open soon," she said, just as if he was arguing, "The housekeeper will be able to get in. You know. Diapers. Real ones."

"That will make life easier," he agreed.

She resented him for being so agreeable, especially since he looked as if he found her amusing, in an annoying sort of way.

"I mean, if things became unmanageable, and the road was open, I could always pack everybody up and go to a motel or something." She realized it was not him she was trying to convince of her competence at all. It was herself!

"Yeah, you could, if the road was open."

"What's the longest the road has been closed?"

He shrugged. "Ten days. That was a washout, though."

"So it should be open soon, right?"

"Momentarily," he agreed.

"All right. I'd better get on with it."

"Uh-huh. Good idea."

She stuck out her hand. "It's been a pleasure meeting you, Major. I really can't thank you enough."

He took her hand. His grip was hard and strong, and she could feel the utter power of him, like an electrical current, pulsing through his hand. His touch made her want to beg him to stay, but not because she needed his help. Because the temptation to explore that electrical feeling between them was almost impossible to turn away from.

Flustered, she grabbed back her hand, ducked her head and consulted her notebook. "Aha," she announced with great authority, as if she had just figured out what task needed to be done first, and whirled away from him.

She pretended not to notice him saying goodbye to the kids, how they clung to him, how they begged him to stay.

She was sure it was not because they didn't have any faith in her, but because they had developed such a strong liking for him.

Well, when the chips were down, it was easy to develop a liking for a rescuer. She was sure there were even names for such attachments.

"Auntie Brooke, tell him he has to stay," Saffron came and begged her, tears standing in her eyes. "You don't know how to look after us all. You just don't."

"Of course I do," she said, insult covering her doubt.

Saffron looked unimpressed and then suspicious. "You didn't tell him to leave, did you?"

"Ah, did he say that?"

"No. He just said it was time for him to go. He said that you would do your best to look after things."

"Well, that's right."

"Auntie Brooke, you look after phones and letters and stuff. You look after Mommy's appointments. You don't know how to do this."

"Yes, I do. And you are going to help me."

Saffron gave her a look, definitely preteen, that was cynical and uncooperative. "I don't want to help *you*," she said and flounced away.

Minutes after Cole had shouldered his backpack and left, the whole team had defected. The children, socks on their heads to ward off the cold, ignored her commands and went upstairs to play. Granny was unresponsive from behind the covers of yet another romance novel.

Only the baby looked at her helpfully.

"No Code Brown until after lunch," the new fearless leader ordered.

Lexandra screwed up her face, turned very red, and then smiled contentedly. A rich aroma wafted off her.

"It's definitely mutiny," Brooke said.

"Definitely," Granny said, not without satisfaction, from behind her book.

By supper time, Brooke was nearly insane. The children were monsters. No matter what she asked them to do, they ignored her. They wouldn't make their beds or help with the dishes. They wouldn't eat the salad she made for lunch, and they wouldn't help with cleanup. They had a water fight in the upstairs bathroom and tramped mud from outside into the front foyer and up the stairs. They fought with each other until Brooke's head ached.

The boys wrapped Kolina, from head to toe, in an entire roll of toilet paper. She was to play the mummy in their game. They didn't care that she didn't want to play. No sooner had Brooke unraveled the tearful Kolina when Saffron appeared in several ghastly layers of her mother's makeup and announced she intended to pierce her own nose with a sewing needle.

Granny wanted her bandage changed forty-six times, and the baby was intent on keeping up with her.

Brooke figured that's why she blew up the grill and caught the house on fire.

Pure mental and physical exhaustion.

She was lighting the grill to cook the few leftover steaks for dinner. The wind came up and blew out the flame. How was she to know the gas just kept running? The wind blew out her next several matches, too. When she finally got one to stay lit, the gas had built up inside the casing of the barbecue. The explosion threw her back against the wall of the house, and she watched in horror as the lid blew right off the barbecue, soared up above the roof of the house, and then crashed into the swampy water of the closed pool.

She turned to see five very frightened faces, and Granny, pressed against the living-room window. Well, at least it had made them all be quiet.

Still shaken, she decided to cook the steaks inside. She wasn't quite sure how to cook over an open fire, but after consulting her notes, she remembered the little bed of coals off to one side. Unfortunately, when she started moving the coals, one of them slipped unnoticed from the fireplace onto the rug.

It was smoldering with astonishing strength when Calypso tugged on her shirt and pointed it out to her. She dumped five gallons of water on it, water that it had taken her the better part of the afternoon to heat. The carpet had to be carted outside and all the mattresses had to be moved so she could mop up soot and water.

It seemed like hours later when they finally ate dry cereal for supper. The children, and Granny, resisted Brooke's efforts to make it a fun part of the adventure.

"It's better than *Survivor*," Brooke insisted with forced cheer.

"No it isn't!" voices chorused back.

And where last night there had been stories and the cheerful flickering of the fire, tonight there was just strained silence.

She waited until the last little person was tucked into bed and Granny was absorbed in her novel before she went out of the warmth of the room and up the stairs to the guest bathroom.

It was cold, and she didn't have a sock to wear on her head. Despite the fact that no one was coming after her, she locked the door. They wouldn't be able to hear her. She closed the seat on the toilet, sat down and cried.

"Ah," Cole said out loud. He stretched his feet out in front of him and regarded the scene he had created with quiet contentment. His own fire threw gentle waves of heat from the fireplace. He had mushrooms sautéing in a pan beside the quietly glowing embers, and a nice rainbow trout sizzled inside foil.

He had heard a truck on the highway earlier, so he knew the road was open. He actually struggled, briefly and not too sincerely, with the idea of going to town and getting some diapers, but no, there was no point. He was not appreciated by Brooke Callan, and he was not going to try to win her over by helping her out. If she was so all fired up to do it on her own, who was he to dissuade her?

He'd have to clear the fallen tree from his own drive-way first, anyway, so the housekeeper could bring diapers when—and if—she showed up.

Cole poured a glass of a very dry red wine from the uncorked bottle on the coffee table in front of him. He sniffed it, swirled it, held it up to the firelight and appreciated the ruby-red glow. It was a lovely moment. His favorite kind of moment. Silent. Serene. No conflict, no chaos, no children, and especially no Brooke Callan.

"Cheers," he said, trying to pretend it didn't sound hollow in his own ears. He put down the wine without tasting it and stared at the fire.

The truth was that he was not enjoying his favorite kind of moment as much as he thought he would, as much as he had just a few days in the past.

"Get real," he reprimanded himself. "I do not miss them. Or her. Unless it's something like missing a tooth-ache once it's finally gone."

One of the realities he had learned from his career choice was that no one was indispensable. One man fell, another took his place. Made do. Figured it out.

Brooke would be doing fine up there. Making do. Figuring it out. Right about now, they were probably all gathered around the fire, finishing the steaks he had left for them, getting ready to tell a story.

He told himself he had no wish to be there. None.

Okay, so he was a little curious about how dinner had turned out and about what kind of story she would tell, but that was all. Maybe Kolina would get her bunnies tonight. Mommy Bunny. Daddy Bunny. Baby Bunny.

PLAY THE
Lucky Key Game

and you can get

FREE BOOKS
and a FREE GIFT!

Do You Have the LUCKY KEY?

Scratch the gold areas with a coin. Then check below to see the books and gift you can get!

YES!
I have scratched off the gold areas. Please send me the **2 FREE BOOKS** and **GIFT** for which I qualify. I understand I am under no obligation to purchase any books, as explained on the back of this card.

309 SDL DVFZ   **209 SDL DVGG**

FIRST NAME	LAST NAME

ADDRESS

APT.#	CITY

STATE/PROV.	ZIP/POSTAL CODE

2 free books plus a free gift   1 free book

2 free books   Try Again!

Visit us online at
www.eHarlequin.com

DETACH AND MAIL CARD TODAY!

(S-R-03/04)

© 2002 HARLEQUIN ENTERPRISES LTD. ® and TM are trademarks owned by Harlequin Books S.A. used under license.

If offer card is missing write to: Silhouette Reader Service, 3010 Walden Ave., P.O. Box 1867, Buffalo NY 14240-1867

BUSINESS REPLY MAIL
FIRST-CLASS MAIL   PERMIT NO. 717-003   BUFFALO, NY

POSTAGE WILL BE PAID BY ADDRESSEE

SILHOUETTE READER SERVICE
3010 WALDEN AVE
PO BOX 1867
BUFFALO NY 14240-9952

NO POSTAGE
NECESSARY
IF MAILED
IN THE
UNITED STATES

Yuck.

Which was how he felt about the wine when he finally tasted it. Could a person develop a taste for grape Kool-Aid? It didn't seem possible, but he forced the cork back into the bottle and set the glass aside. He was not much of a drinker, and one of the reasons was that he liked control.

One glass of wine and he might be tempted to explore more deeply the reason eating this fish alone was not quite the experience he wanted it to be.

He had polished off most of the fish when he heard it. A tiny tap on his front door. He leaped to his feet so quickly he knocked the wine bottle off the coffee table. He wondered, uneasily, if he might have been waiting for that very sound. He went to the door without picking up the bottle.

He opened the door, expecting Brooke. Considering he had put the wine away with barely a sip, it occurred to him he was thinking woozily because he entertained the completely irrational thought that, if it was her, he was going to take both her wrists, pull her hard into him and cover her mouth with his own.

He felt a sharp stab of disappointment that it was Saffron who stood there, one of his socks pulled over her head, a warm winter jacket around her.

"She blew the lid off the barbecue," she announced sadly, without saying hello. "And lit the rug on fire."

Somehow there was no need to ask who.

"Is everyone all right?" He took those small shoulders between his hands and looked Saffron right in the eye. "Is Brooke hurt? Any of the children?"

"Not yet," Saffron said, "but give her time."

But no, he wasn't giving her time. She'd had her chance. Cole packed a few things in his backpack, swung Saffron onto his shoulders and began the now-familiar trek through the woods.

He tried to convince himself he was irritated. He tried to feel smug. Hadn't he guessed something like this might happen?

But in actual fact, what he felt stirring deep inside himself was not crankiness. It felt suspiciously like happiness. And not because she had failed.

But because he was needed.

He felt like a man who had been searching for his way home for a long long time and finally found it.

But that would have to be his closely guarded secret. How annoying that it had popped into his head even after he had resisted the wine. *In vino veritas.* But the truth had arrived without the help of the wine.

He arrived to find a soaked rug, charred badly on one corner, out on the front step. The children were huddled around Granny in the great room, the fire limping along.

No Brooke.

"Thank God," Granny said. "Welcome home."

He went past her and put some wood on the fire. *Home.* This was not his home. Granny was joking. And yet the word evoked some deep longing, a hidden wish within him.

"She's in the upstairs bathroom," Darrance told him, making Cole wonder, uneasily, if his concern for Brooke had shown on his face. "I think she's slitting her wrists."

"Because of the rug?" Cole said. She did worry about *stuff.* Rugs, towels, sheets. He thought again about kissing her. That would chase her damn stuff obsession right out of her mind.

And cause a new and worrisome obsession for him.

If he tasted those lips once, would it be enough? He doubted it.

No more wine, he told himself, not so much as a drop. Not until he had negotiated the tricky terrain of this mission.

"Maybe she's upset because of the rug," Darrance said, but Cole caught a certain evasive note in the boy's tone, in his suddenly skittering eyes.

He gave Darrance his sternest look. "Maybe?"

"We were a little bit naughty today. Especially Calypso. Making Kolina into the mummy was his stupid idea."

"Wapped in toilet paper," Kolina informed him, tears coming to her eyes, not missing a chance to get her brothers in trouble.

"It wasn't my idea," Calypso yelled at Darrance. "Liar! You're a big, fat snoogy!"

What kind of fool has five children? Cole wondered, but affectionately. He held up his hand. "I'll be back to deal with you," he said sternly, and the boys exchanged worried looks.

He went up the stairs and through the chilly house. He followed the sounds of sobbing through a guest bedroom and to the bathroom door. Sobbing. Good God in heaven. He was a rough soldier. What did he know about crying women?

He knocked lightly on the door.

The sobbing was choked back.

"Saffron, I'm fine," she called, trying to insert cheer into the hoarseness of her voice. "I just need a few minutes to myself."

"It's not Saffron. Open the door."

Silence.

"I mean it, Brooke, open the door."

"Or what?" she asked. Geez, still defiant.

"Or I'll break it down. One more thing to explain to your boss, along with the wrecked rug and the barbecue in the pool, the sheets and the towels."

"Just the lid is in the pool. And the rug can be repaired. They like Persian rugs to look a little lived-in, anyway. They actually put them out on the street in Turkish markets and let people walk on them, to achieve that nice worn look."

He was not about to be put off with trivia. "You've achieved the worn look, all right. Worn by a tribe of fire-walkers. Open the door."

She opened it a crack, peered defiantly out at him. "So, you don't think the rug can be repaired?"

"I could care less about the stupid rug. I'm not here to talk about the rug."

"Why are you here? Never mind! I know! To rub my nose in the fact I've made a shambles of everything."

He pushed open the door. She did not put up any kind of fight, which told him quite a lot about her day. The impulse to kiss her was stronger. That would chase the defensiveness away, but he was a man not given to impulses and he resisted this one. "To make sure you're all right."

"Fine," she said. "You can see I'm fine."

Her face was blotchy from crying. Her outfit looked as if it had been expensive suede once upon a time. It fit her beautifully. But now it was wet and streaked with soot and baby puke. Her hair had fallen free of the ponytail. Her pulse beat in her throat, rapid, like a terrified rabbit.

He felt the impulse again, stronger, to cover her lips with his own. He thwarted it by touching her cheek, pushing a strand of wayward hair back from her face and tucking it behind her ear.

"So now you can go away." He could tell she didn't mean it. She had not even slapped his hand away from her hair. If he was a more intuitive kind of guy, maybe he would have realized that this morning. That she hadn't really wanted him to go.

Why had he come? He had a weakness for tempting fate. He'd spent most of his life at it. But he wasn't going to admit he was back of his own accord, drawn here by an invisible but powerful thread. "Saffron came and got me."

"By herself? At night?" She looked as if she was going to start crying again.

"That doesn't matter now."

"Doesn't it?"

He shook his head. "All that matters now is that I'm here. And I'm staying."

She lifted her chin defiantly, apparently thought about arguing, but then her chin fell. She looked down and plucked at a button on the ruined shirt. "All right."

"Don't be so hard on yourself," he heard himself saying. He lifted her chin, made her look directly into his eyes. "It does not mean you are a failure as a human being. Because you caught the rug on fire."

"And blew up the barbecue," she added morosely.

"Just the lid," he reminded her and that coaxed a small smile out of her. "Come on. Let's start over. I'm Major Cole Standen. You can call me Cole. I am a professional rescuer." He stuck out his hand. "Been doing it all my life. It's what I'm best at."

"Brooke Callan," she said, "damsel-in-distress. It seems to be what I'm best at, too."

And then they were both laughing.

"Doing it all your life?" he asked her between chuckles.

"So it seems," she said and accepted his hand.

It should have been a quick, hard shake. But her hand lingered, and he did not pull his away.

He had been on rescue missions and adventures his entire life.

But this was different.

This was going to be an adventure of the heart. And Cole Standen could not for the life of him say if he was happy or sorry.

Chapter Five

"I need to change," Brooke stammered. She looked down at herself and blushed crimson. And not, he guessed, because of the soot and baby puke. She crossed her arms defensively over her chest. "I'm wet."

Yes, he could see that. What had he done to deserve the fact he was always going to see her wet when it would be most ungentlemanly to take advantage of it?

Because she was not just wet, but vulnerable, something no gentleman would take advantage of.

Not that he had ever considered himself much of a gentleman. His military career had been without glamour. The dress greens and social functions had been minimal. He had never had any of the kinds of political or career aspirations that might make a person brush up on his manners.

Cole had prided himself on being a hands-on kind of leader. It meant he had never asked a man to do something he was not willing to do himself. It meant getting dirty and bruised and ending some days so tired he swayed on his feet. What he'd liked best about his job was that it challenged him, daily, to be stronger, smarter and faster.

But suddenly, facing the temptation of Brooke Callan, he expected more of himself. He wanted to be better than he had ever been before. More, somehow. And he wanted to bring out the best in her, instead of the worst, as he had done so far.

Cole had led men in terrible and tough situations where the unexpected could unfold at an alarming rate, and the consequences could be brutal. The gift from that was that he knew when somebody had made a bad mistake they were at their most vulnerable. It was not victory that brought people to turning points in their lives. It was defeat. In the painful and delicate time spent in the no-man's-land of remorse, regret and self-questioning a person could be crushed—or they could be helped to grow and profit from error.

He had heard a story, early in his career, about Thomas Edison. That story had become his guidepost when dealing with people struggling with the consequences of bad decisions, human errors or slips in judgment.

Edison, on his way to a press conference to reveal his new invention, the lightbulb, had handed his prototype to a young assistant. Nervous about being singled out for such a great honor, the young man dropped the lightbulb and it shattered. Edison went quietly back to work, re-created the lightbulb, and when it was time to unveil it the second time, he singled out the very same young man to carry it for him.

Brooke had dropped the lightbulb. She had something to prove with her great bid for independence this morning, and she had failed to prove it.

"How about if I bring you up some warm water?" he suggested, easing his way toward a truce, a partnership that he hoped would bring out the best in both of them instead of the worst. "You can get cleaned up, and then we'll come up with a game plan for the next little while."

He could see she was astonished, and slightly taken aback, by the *we*. She studied him, looking for a motive.

"Please don't be nice to me," she said, tilting her head proudly. "I was very nasty this morning. And stupid. I tossed you out on a point of pride, and I endangered the children by doing it."

"Yeah, that's true."

She gave him a flustered frown, inviting him to take her to task, rake her over the coals, dress her down. When he did not accept the invitation, she fed him a little more ammunition. "I nearly blew myself up and burned down the house."

"*Nearly* can be a fairly important measure," he pointed out calmly. "The house is still here and so are you."

"But you knew I was inviting catastrophe when I asked you to leave. You knew things could go very wrong."

"Actually, my imagination isn't good enough to come up with all the things that really did go wrong. I thought you'd kind of bumble your way through. Had I known the truth, you couldn't have gotten me out of here with a cattle prod."

"So you won't be leaving again?"

"Not a chance."

She had the humility to look relieved. "That's a little better," she said with a small smile. "Though you could have told me this morning I was making a mistake."

"Would you have listened?" He could feel a smile beginning.

"Of course not. I would have thought you had branded me a helpless female, the kind I despise the most, by the way. And I would have branded you a fearmonger at best and an autocratic monster at worst."

"An autocratic monster," he said with a sad shake of his head. "I'm glad I left when I did."

"You know, this would be so much easier for me if you would be disagreeable."

"I know."

"Okay, don't make it easy for me." She looked at her feet, glanced back at him. "I'm sorry," she said softly.

"We all make mistakes, Brooke."

"Somehow I can't imagine you do."

If she had any clue what he was thinking about her lips, she'd know how incredibly wrong she was!

"Let me bring that water."

She laughed, and it was a real laugh. It lightened the anxious look on her face, made her glow with wholesome beauty. "That would be so nice. If we had any warm water. I used it to put out the fire. And it had taken so damn long to heat, I hesitated before I used it! I could have—"

"Let's not go any further down the *could have* road. We'll just scratch the offer for warm water. Get yourself into something dry—" and please, God, not too sexy "—and we'll get these kids organized for bed."

He went downstairs and did a quick inventory. No warm water. Very little wood. The towels in short supply. Supper dishes, such as they were, had not been cleared away. The mattresses were in a jumble and an inordinate amount of toys had been collecting in the room. Granny peevishly reported they had been forced to eat dry cereal for supper.

He lined the kids up tallest to smallest. There was no mistaking the relief in their small faces that someone was taking charge. They looked worn right out from running the show all day. And from running Brooke ragged. After making it clear he was not hearing all their various and sundry complaints about the day, he gave them each a job.

"Darrance and Saffron, get flashlights and gather firewood, branches about as thick as my arm. The woods are full of them from the windstorm. Just enough for the fire tonight. Put on whistles and don't ever get out of sight of each other or the house. Report back in fifteen minutes."

"Aye, aye, sir," they said, nearly stumbling over each other in their enthusiasm to obey. Darrance apparently thought he was off the hook for his naughtiness earlier. Not likely.

"Calypso, you can come with me. We'll work on the barbecue." Calypso swelled with pride to be chosen, possibly thinking he was off the hook for mummifying his sister, too.

"Me job," Kolina said. Today she was dressed in a red flannel nightie with—surprise—Dalmatians cavorting all over it. She had one of his woolen socks on her head, pulled over her ears, and she looked adorable. Simply put, she'd grown on him. All these kids had.

"I saved the most important job for you," he said, getting down on one knee and looking her right in the eye. "You need to stack all the toys over there."

"Not mine," she protested prettily, batting her eyelashes at him.

"And when you're done," he said, resisting her

charms but not easily, "then you get to pick the story for tonight. Do you have storybooks in your room?"

She nodded eagerly.

"Up to your room and back, collect a storybook, no detours. I was thinking something with bunnies would be good."

"Oh, bunnies," Kolina breathed rapturously and scampered away.

"Granny, you're in charge of the baby and the fire."

"Aye, aye, sir."

"How did you do that?" Brooke asked from the doorway. "Charm Kolina so completely? The best I got from her today was a sullen look and a word she's not supposed to know, let alone say."

"Believe me, I have to work overtime to keep from being charmed right around that little one's finger. She's going to be dangerous someday."

Speaking of dangerous, he tried not to stare at Brooke. He did not know how long she had been standing there, but she looked like a different woman than the one he had found near collapse a short while ago, different from the woman who had been so determined to be unattractive yesterday, even different from how she had first appeared, bedraggled and lopsided, on the doorstep.

He'd always suspected this great capacity for true beauty was there, lingering just below the surface.

. She was dressed in hip-hugging jeans that made her look as long-legged and slender as a spring colt. The white sweater was also form-hugging, the V at the neck hinting at the nicest cleavage. She had brushed her hair until it shone and left it hanging loose around her shoulders. It looked as if she had added just a touch of makeup. Her eyes looked huge, her cheekbones amazing, and her lips as though she had just licked them.

"Getting there," Granny said approvingly, voicing the thoughts that he dared not speak out loud.

He reminded himself he had to restore order first. Then work at restoring Brooke's confidence. He was not sure where kissing her until she screamed for mercy fit into that picture. It probably didn't.

"Warm water is probably our first priority," he said, forcing his mind back on track. "And if you could get those dishes out of the way, I'll maybe cook up the rest of those steaks before they spoil."

"I'm sure everybody's hungry," Brooke conceded. "We didn't have much for supper."

"Cheerios without milk," Granny told him and looked very much as though she planned to elaborate on each of the fiascoes that had occurred during the day.

He didn't have a private moment to brief her on the Thomas Edison method of character building, so Cole gave her a quick and quelling look that said he'd heard enough.

Rather than looking chastened, Granny grinned at him with fiendish delight, like a cat who had swallowed a canary.

Cole took Calypso and they went outside. He got the lifesaving hook down and got the small boy to try to pick the barbecue lid out of the murky water of the shut-down pool. Out of the corner of Cole's eye he made sure Calypso didn't get too enthusiastic about his lid-retrieving duties, while he checked out the damage to the grill.

Despite the detachment of the lid, it did not look nearly as bad as he had imagined it would. The pressure all seemed to have blown upward and the body of the barbecue was remarkably undamaged. Cole checked and tightened all the connections. He started it once, and it hissed nicely to life. Then, thoughtful, he turned it off and went to the door.

"Brooke?"

She appeared and looked askance at him.

"Come on. We'll try lighting the barbecue again."

She shrank back from him. "No. Really. I'm busy." She held up her tea towel. "See?"

It was no time to wheedle, argue or discuss. "Outside, now," he said, packing twenty years of cold authority into the order.

Her mouth opened and closed, then opened again. She thought of at least a dozen arguments and each flitted through the expressiveness of her eyes. But she didn't speak them. She took a deep breath, set down the towel and came toward him.

This is what he knew: the human spirit could be a fragile thing. A human spirit could be scarred, even altered, by mishaps like falls from horses, or broken light-bulbs, or blown-up barbecues. Something that seemed small, almost insignificant, could grow over the years as a mind played with it, turned it over, elaborated on it. Fear could break the human spirit.

The wisdom of getting back on the horse after the spill was well known. The same principle applied to barbecues.

So he showed her the barbecue. He explained how it worked. He explained how she had managed to blow the lid off it and how to prevent future explosions. He showed her how to check all the connections for tightness and gas leaks.

She smelled good. Not of perfume, but of soap, and something else subtle and sweet that he could only think was the smell of a woman.

Finally, he gave her the matches and went into the

house, supposedly to retrieve the steaks but mostly to let her have this moment of facing her fear all by herself.

He watched from the kitchen window. He could see she was trembling as she contemplated the barbecue. She shot a worried look at Calypso. For a moment he thought maybe he had misjudged her. But then she took a deep breath and turned the valve to release the propane. She shut it off again quickly, took another deep breath, and then struck the match.

She opened the valve, the barbecue flickered un-eventfully to life, and she laughed out loud. And then she caught him looking at her from the window.

He came back out with the platter full of steaks as if nothing had happened. She acted as if nothing had happened.

But they both knew something important had occurred.

She passed him back the matches, her hand touching his, pausing, and then she moved quickly away.

She went and knelt on the edge of the pool with Calypso, giving Cole a great and awe-inspiring view of the way those jeans stretched over perfect curves.

Cole caught a glimpse of who she really was as she leaned out over the pool, trying to snag the lid with the hook. She was so fully alive, laughing, calling playful instructions. Unable to reach the lid, even with the hook, she devised several improbable plans. Finally, she splashed water toward the lid creating a little wave for it to ride over to Calypso.

If she wasn't careful, she was going to get wet again. Darn. She finally persuaded the lid out of the center of the pool, and Calypso snatched it up. They bore it over to him like championship hockey players carrying their trophy.

Cole reattached it, suddenly aware that Brooke was as aware of him as he was of her. He could not resist the juvenile impulse to flex his muscles unnecessarily as he put the lid back on and was satisfied with what he saw on her face.

Brooke stared at the muscle that leaped in Cole's arm as he reattached the barbecue lid. He was a beautifully made man. But more than being beautifully made, she was catching glimpse after glimpse of a beautiful spirit.

She licked her lips, caught him looking at her and looked away. She thought of something that needed doing in the house.

Like a hose to put out the fire on her cheeks. But in the house she contemplated what Cole Standen was really asking of her.

He was asking her to trust him.

More, he was asking her to trust herself. And not just with barbecues. He was asking her to dig inside herself and find out what was really there.

She was far more afraid to do that than she had been to hold that fluttering match to the hissing barbecue again. But she'd done it. She had overcome her fear and moved ahead.

Could that lesson be applied to other parts of her life? Did she want it to?

It was late by the time they all sat around the fire, contentedly munching steak. Brooke shared the hearth with Cole, aware of the hard muscle of his thigh touching hers. She could have moved away, but she didn't, and she realized it was one way of saying yes, to trusting him, to trusting herself.

"This is better than cereal," Saffron said to Brooke, her tone not at all kind.

"It might not have been cereal if any one of you had listened to me," Brooke said casually, her eyes closed as she savored her steak and the scent wafting off the man beside her.

It was more than barbecue sauce and smoke. He smelled rich and clean and strong, an aroma she could only identify as the smell of a man.

She became aware of uncomfortable silence and opened her eyes to see no one was savoring the aroma of steak and man except her. The kids were all looking at her with wide, pleading eyes.

"No one listened to Brooke?" Cole said much too casually.

"Me did," Kolina said angelically.

"No, you didn't!" Saffron said. "When Brooke told you to stop jumping on the couch with your muddy feet, you stuck your tongue out at her and said poo-poo head. Only you didn't say poo-poo."

"I'm sure you're mistaken, Saffron," Brooke said.

"I am not!"

"Wapped in toilet paper," Kolina reminded Cole desperately. "Poor Kolina."

"You weren't any better, Saffron," Darrance said. "You were putting on Mom's makeup instead of helping with lunch, and then you said you were going to pierce your nose. With a knitting needle."

"A sewing needle," she corrected him tartly, then sent him a murderous look when she realized he had walked her into an admission of guilt.

"We all knew you weren't going to pierce your nose, Saffron," Brooke said. She glanced at Cole. He had lowered his eyebrows, and his eyes were closed to slits as he regarded one storyteller and then the next. He was very intimidating, and the quieter he was the more the children talked—each trying to redeem themselves at the expense of a brother or sister.

Saffron shot Brooke a grateful look, but she wasn't done with her brother. "You were the worst one, Darrance. You tracked all that mud in the front door and went up and down the stairs and just pretended you couldn't hear, even when Brooke was shrieking at you."

"Not shrieking," Brooke protested. "Not exactly."

"Exactly!" Darrance said, in a black mood now.

But it didn't matter what she said, the kids were bent now on each getting the other one in more trouble.

Cole sat stone-faced, listening, and she thought, from the sternness of his expression, that he was really angry at the children. But then she felt the quiver of his shoulder where it touched hers, and when she turned and looked at him she saw his mouth twitching suspiciously with contained mirth as the stories got wilder and more accusatory.

Finally, he held up his hand.

"I've heard enough. You were all naughty. Every single one of you, with the possible exceptions of Granny and Lexy."

Brooke saw Granny trying not to look too guilty given how she had enjoyed the mutiny of the children.

"Lexy wasn't that good," Calypso said. "She Code Browned. And puked. Do we have a code for that?"

"Not yet," Cole said. "You know, I have to tell you all I'm very disappointed in you. You needed to pull together as a team, and you didn't."

The children looked crushed.

"You were nasty to Brooke, and all she wanted to do was help you."

Kolina began to cry.

Cole picked her up, and she tucked herself into him,

slurping on her thumb, peeping out at her brothers and sisters with sly satisfaction.

"So," he said, "what do you think I should do about it?"

"Spankings," Kolina said, removing her thumb from her mouth. "Them. Not me." She put her thumb back in her mouth.

"Well, I can see why every now and then they want to mummify you," Cole said. "And I don't do spankings."

His shoulder was still shaking, especially at the relieved looks on the faces of his captive audience.

"Any other suggestions?"

"No bunny stories. Them. Me still have bunny stories," Kolina said.

"Ah, I think I've heard enough suggestions from you," Cole said. "Anyone else?"

"You could ground us," Saffron said with just a touch too much eagerness.

"What does that mean?"

"No phone calls. No TV. No CD player."

"We have no power," he reminded her. "We don't have any of those things."

"Oh." She tried to look as if that came as a surprise to her.

"Darrance?"

"You could make us run with forty-pound packs. Like in the army." Darrance actually sounded hopeful.

"If you carried the baby and Kolina that would be about forty pounds," Cole said dryly. "Still game?"

Darrance shook his head.

"How about you, Calypso? Any ideas?"

"Yeah. Let's tie Darrance to a tree and take turns

hitting him with a stick. And then when we're done with him—''

''That's okay. We've heard enough from you,'' Cole said hastily. ''Brooke, did you want to say anything?''

She shook her head. If she opened her mouth all that was going to come out was laughter.

He rolled his eyes. ''Okay. This is what I think. Tonight, you all have to apologize for the hard time you gave Brooke.'' He held up his hand when they all started agreeing eagerly. ''And tomorrow, all of you have to wait on Brooke. Breakfast in bed, Kool-Aid anytime she snaps her fingers. And you guys look after the Code Browns.''

They were suddenly, fiercely silent.

''Agreed?'' he asked.

''Agreed,'' they muttered one after another.

''Great.'' He moved on swiftly. ''Kolina has picked a bedtime story for us. It's called *Mr. Bunny's Baby, Barney.*''

''Is this part of the punishment?'' Calypso asked, but he gathered just as close as the rest of them.

''Saffron, could you read it?'' Cole said, then got up rapidly and left the room.

If she went after him, it would be like saying yes to trusting him, to trusting herself, to trusting life.

''I'll be right back,'' Brooke said, having to bite her tongue enough that it hurt to keep the laughter from bubbling out.

She chased Cole out of the room. He was standing in the hall trying to smother his laughter. He straightened and regarded her thoughtfully for a moment, knowing full well what she was saying yes to.

He grabbed her hand and pulled her out the front door and across the lawn.

And when he was far enough away from the house, he threw back his head and howled with laughter. And so did she. They laughed until they were bent over double. And when one of them showed signs of slowing down, the other would say, "Me still have bunny stories,"or "You could ground us."

Finally, he threw his arm over her shoulder, and they walked back to the house. His arm felt good over her shoulder, strong and warm and as if it belonged there.

"Are you sure you can go back in there with a straight face?" he demanded at the door.

"Oh, yeah, as long as you don't say, let's tie Darrance to a tree and hit him with sticks."

They started laughing again, trying to stifle it. They had to wait a few more minutes before they went back in.

An hour later, Brooke and Cole sat on the couch together, the last restless shuffling having died out as the children settled on their mattresses. She had received a gracious and heartfelt apology from each of them. Kolina had written her a note that said: BABCKM, with a big heart around it. Kolina informed her solemnly that it said, "I love you better than bunnies, and I never be bad again." Brooke thought she would probably keep it forever.

"How do you do it?" Brooke asked Cole, feeling so companionable, loving the solidness of his company so much. Was she mistaken, or did he bring out the best in her? "Why do they listen to you and not to me?"

"Long years of practice. Pick out the ringleader. In this case Saffron. Win her, you win them all."

"There's got to be more to it than that."

He shrugged. "It's been scientifically proven that kids

and animals respond to male voices with more respect than female ones. It makes the feminists crazy, but it's just nature.''

"They want to listen to you. They are dying for you to approve of them.''

He looked out over the sea of small sleeping bodies and smiled. That smile, faintly tender, made him so handsome. It was a memory she would savor forever, just like Kolina's note.

''I've been in the leadership business for a lot of years,'' he said. ''Some of the young men I've worked with really haven't seemed that much older than these kids, sadly enough.''

"The kids don't just respect you. They adore you. They hated me.''

''No, they didn't. They sized you up, decided you weren't scary and bucked you every inch of the way. Every drill sergeant and old schoolteacher knows the same trick—you start out mean as a rattlesnake. You can soften it up later, but you can't turn on the mean later. It's too late.''

"So, it's too late for me to get mean?''

''You started off mean with me,'' he said approvingly. ''Now you can be nice. I know you're made of steel under all that soft beauty.''

She laughed. ''I'm not beautiful.''

''No?''

''You want to see beautiful? Wait until you see Shauna.'' Even though she kept her tone light, Brooke felt the little ache of fear in her breast when she said that. All this trust stuff was just fine, but the truth was that it had not been tested. Yet.

''I think I had the pleasure. Last summer. On my beach.''

"And?"

He shrugged.

"Come on."

"Look, I don't want to say bad things about your boss."

Bad things? About Shauna? Of course, she knew all about the incident on the beach, but she was inordinately interested in hearing about it from his perspective. It was a rare thing, indeed, to find someone who could stand up to Shauna. It gave her a small hope that maybe Shauna's impossible two-part test could be passed.

"Just between you and me," she promised.

"She was lying on my beach right underneath a No Trespassing sign. That didn't apply to her, apparently. She had her top undone, and she had on makeup and false fingernails. Her hair had been styled. She just seemed about as real as a three-dollar bill. And like a spoiled brat." He chuckled. "But even all that makeup couldn't hide the fact she was turning a hideous shade of purple when her husband dragged her back to the canoe. I got the impression the woman hasn't heard the word *no* nearly enough in her life."

He had practically passed the first test then! He had resisted Shauna! Still, she'd been with Milton and not really trying to test Cole in *that* way. Brooke could not help but feel cynical. "Come on. No one in the world can resist her."

"If you say so," he said. "That's what she seemed to think, too. That she should have the run of *my* beach because she looks great in a bikini and knows how to bat her eyelashes." He laughed. "Come to think of it, Kolina comes by it honestly."

"Well, Shauna has the run of the rest of the world because of that! Famous people do get what they want."

She suddenly felt guilty about discussing her boss. "She really is a fine actress."

"That's good," he said without much interest. "I like real myself, but each to their own."

Real. What Brooke had known instantly and intuitively Cole Standen was. She tried to evaluate if she was real or not, in his eyes. It was a little hard to believe that one attribute—real—could stand up to the glamour of Shauna.

"Have you seen any of her movies?" If he had, he probably would be much more susceptible to her charms.

"You'd laugh at how few movies I've seen. The last one was, uh, *Dances with Wolves*. I don't have much in the way of imagination. I have trouble with make-believe. It just didn't work in my world."

Suddenly, Shauna and her world did seem a very long way away. And what Brooke wanted most was to know his reality. "Tell me about your world."

"Nah."

"No, really."

He shot her a surprised look, hesitated, and then closed his eyes. She saw, suddenly, how very lonely he was.

And then he surprised her by beginning to speak. His voice soft, he took her to places she had never been. Real places. Worlds torn apart. He told her stories of courage, hardship and heartbreak. He told her of the triumph of the human spirit in appalling conditions.

He stopped, suddenly, embarrassed. "Sorry. I'm boring you."

"Not at all." And she meant it. Rather than being bored she felt entranced by this side of the man.

He changed the subject, and she saw he was not used

to speaking about himself. "So did all the kids get names from their mother's movies?"

"Yes. Aren't they wonderful?"

"Hmmph. Saffron sounds like a kind of chicken I had in India en route to Africa, and Calypso seems to have a little fascination with violence that could probably be attributed to having to defend himself at school."

"They don't go to school. Not traditional school. They video link."

"It just gets worse and worse."

"They could never have a normal school experience. Not with their mother being who she is."

"No, I guess not."

"You don't approve."

"Does it matter whether I do or not?"

"I guess I'd just like to know what you think."

"I think kids should have normal childhoods. School. Baseball teams. Summer camp."

"That's why she bought this place. Woods. The great outdoors. It's a secret. No cameras in the kids' faces. No tabloid reporters. She even tries not to have too much staff. She doesn't want her children raised by strangers."

"It seems like a bit more than her aging mother is up to," he said, his voice suddenly low, since they were both aware the aging mother was probably listening avidly.

"Usually there is a housekeeper here during the day. And a nanny."

"She needs security."

Brooke felt a sinking sensation. "And you'd be perfect for the job, right?"

He didn't even open his eyes. "Nah. I'm retired. And way too cranky."

But if he was put to the test would he mean that, or could he be tempted?

She was suddenly too exhausted for this last question. She had put up with rebelling children, nearly blown herself up and caught the house on fire. She had asked herself the most difficult questions about trust.

That was enough for one day, and now, having listened to some of his stories, it felt as though she was putting her heart at risk.

"I'm going to bed," she said and got up off the couch. He caught her wrist. His eyes were open, far more alert than she had thought they would be.

He tugged her, and she wobbled and then fell forward slightly. Just enough for him to reach up and graze his lips against hers.

She pulled back from him, stunned.

That smallest touch of his lips had been electrical, far more frightening than either the blowup of the barbecue or the fire on the rug.

"What did you do that for?" she whispered, touching her lips. Could it be possible they still tingled?

"I wanted to know what you tasted like," he whispered back.

They both heard a stifled cackle. Brooke gave him one more quick glance before she scrambled away and got under her own blankets, completely dressed.

Even though she was exhausted, sleep would not come. He had kissed her. She had been horrible to him, and a terrible failure, and tonight his lips had said none of that mattered.

It felt as if he saw her, when no one else ever had. The real Brooke Callan.

This couldn't be happening to her. And yet she could not deny that she was so happy it was. Though she would have been a whole lot happier if her relationship with Cole Standen was unfolding without Granny's scrutiny. Could it really be called a relationship? Isn't that what kisses meant? Relationships?

"Try the pink negligee tomorrow," Granny whispered.

Brooke clamped her eyes shut and pretended to be fast asleep. But it was as though she could still feel his lips and taste them, sweet as wild strawberries.

She shivered. Could he really pass the Shauna test?

Chapter Six

Cole Standen lay on the couch. He decided it was damn uncomfortable and blamed that for the insomnia that plagued him. He was a man who had slept, with perfect ease, on canvas cots, in hard, rocky places and on the desert floor, but it was easier to blame the couch for his sleeplessness than to look at the truth.

He had kissed her.

Not the wild, hungry kiss he had wanted.

A gentle kiss. A greeting. A kiss that had left him dissatisfied, yearning for more. Because that kiss had confirmed part of what he knew.

The kiss had tasted of wild honey, and indeed, that was what she was, sweet and untamed at the same time. Complex and simple. Innocent and seductive. Brooke Callan was just one mystifying delightful contradiction after another.

He knew her better than he should after such a short acquaintance. But emergencies did that. Showed you what was at the core of a person, in their heart and soul.

He could also tell a great deal about her from how she interacted with the children. She wanted the world to believe she was the hard-bitten executive type, but children and dogs could always scent out a person's true character. The children had pegged her sweetness, and the little devils had been quick to take advantage of it, too.

He asked himself a zillion questions—what had she been like as a child? What had made her choose the career she had chosen? But he carefully avoided the question that was trying to get his attention.

Where was all this going? Besides around and around in his head. Finally, he slept, but he had experienced better sleeps in places where machine guns went off all night.

Cole awoke in the morning to the now-familiar sight of Kolina's big blue eyes just inches from his face.

She smiled, absolutely delighted that he had decided to join her in the land of wakefulness. A few days ago he would not have guessed he was the kind of man a child would delight in.

"Mr. Bunny?" she said hopefully, holding the book up for him.

He felt as though he had a hangover, and it would be much easier to blame Mr. Bunny than that woman over there. He glanced over. Brooke was wrapped up in her blankets, like a sausage in a roll. Her cheek had the pattern of the pillow imprinted into it. Her hair was in wild disarray, and that bit of makeup she had put on yesterday was now smudged under her eyes.

She looked beautiful. Far more beautiful than her boss could ever look.

"Mr. Bunny?" Kolina pressed. "Pwee?"

Who could resist that? So he read Mr. Bunny and

watched his little encampment wake up one by one. But he especially watched Brooke, the fluttering of her lashes, the sigh and yawn, the stretch. Her eyes opened reluctantly and closed again instantly. Caught between sleep and wakefulness, she frowned, pulled the pillow over her head.

He couldn't think of one single sight he would rather wake up to. He noticed she was peeking out from under the pillow at him, and he winked. She disappeared back under the pillow.

The thing about trying to conduct a romance in the presence of five children and a granny was that you couldn't! Someone was watching all the time. There was always a string of demands. This needed to be done and that, and there was really—thank God—absolutely no time for exploring the mysteries of her eyes.

A romance? It was his turn to frown. The word *romance* was really not in his vocabulary. But it did answer the question that he had not yet voiced.

Was that where this was going? A romance? Surely, nothing so formal. A friendship? A partnership?

His eyes lingered on her lips. Nope. A romance. He wanted to romance her.

"As if," he muttered to himself. Romancing her would require a decision of life-altering proportions. A romance, a relationship, wasn't just something you stumbled into by accident. Was it?

"Doesn't say that as if," Kolina said, annoyed since she had every single word of the book memorized.

"No, it doesn't," he said, taken aback by the mutinous turn his own mind was taking. Romance, and the other R word, were for younger men. Men who had the energy for it. Men who knew about flowers and small talk, wining and dining and dancing. Frankly, everything on that list made him cringe.

Why don't you just surrender? a voice inside him asked. See where it goes, see where it leads?

Because that was not how he had led his life. His life had been a series of planned events, controlled. The word *surrender,* like the two R words, had not been in his vocabulary.

Not until a few days ago, when those children had knocked on his door. But maybe it had not been just children knocking on his door. It had been life knocking, telling him to get back in the game, taking pity on a man so lonely he did not even have the sense to know how alone he was, not until a ready-made family was dumped on his doorstep.

A little family that made him crave things he had not craved, want things he had not wanted. Who would have guessed the laughter of children could warm a heart so thoroughly? Who would have guessed a baby's puddled warmth against a man's chest made his life feel as though it had some meaning it had not had before?

Who would have guessed looking at a woman, smelling her, brushing your thigh against her thigh, could make a man feel so alive? So full of hope, so aware of the possibilities each new day held?

It all seemed to lead right back to her lips.

With one final glance, he made himself get up and begin breakfast. She had hopped into bed fully clothed last night, and now she hopped out the same way and came to help him. She was rumpled, her hair was a mess, her makeup was smudged, and he liked it all. He liked getting breakfast ready and watching her growing authority with the children.

"This baby needs a bath," she announced after the

breakfast things had been cleared away. "Not just a sponging off, a bath."

"Have at," he said. "Bathing babies is not my department at all."

"And why not?" she said, folding her arms over her chest and tapping her foot.

A fighting stance if he had ever seen one. He held up his hands. "These hands strip rifles and change flat tires and chop wood and put worms on hooks. Men things."

She was looking at his hands with a strange hunger burning in her eyes, a hunger that made him realize his hands wanted to explore all kinds of softer territory.

"It's a two-person job," she said firmly. "Wet babies are slippery."

He knew, suddenly, that just as he had helped her face the challenge of her fears, she was now asking him to explore new territory, move out of his comfort zone, challenge himself.

"I found out all about slippery babies on night one. And she was the worst kind of slippery. Oozing slippery stuff out the sides to be exact." It was a token protest. He already knew they were going to be bathing the baby together.

"Well, then, this should be a piece of cake for you, Major."

"Okay, okay," he said, pretending exasperation. But when Brooke looked at him, grinning, he knew she had seen he was saying yes to more than bathing a baby.

It went a long way toward taking away that feeling of being alone in the world when someone saw the things you didn't say.

"Okay," Brooke said a short while later, kneeling in front of the warmth of the fire with an amazing assortment of items around her. "Tub."

"Check," he said, looking dubiously at the plastic bucket she had found somewhere. Clean, but sturdy enough to hold a baby?

"Baby soap," she said.

Retrieved from the nursery, the soap smelled of innocence and hope, of generations of loving mothers cleaning their babies.

Mothers. "Actually, Saffron should help you with this. I'll just call—"

"If you abandon me now, I'll call your old regiment and expose you as a chicken."

He slid her a look. She wasn't kidding.

"Towel," she said, holding it up. "One of three remaining in the entire house."

"Check."

"Clean sleepers."

The sleepers were tiny and soft and the color of candy floss. "Check."

"Baby powder, petroleum jelly, hair ribbon. We're ready," she declared. She poured warm water into the tub and tested it on her wrist. "You try it."

He tried it. It seemed okay to him, but his skin was tough, leathery, not like that baby's skin. "I'll defer to you on water temperature."

"It's perfect," she decided. It took both of them to get those wildly flapping limbs out of the sleeper the baby was in. Lexy cooed with delight as she hit the water.

Well, that answered the sturdiness-of-the-container question and the water temperature question. The baby was slippery as Jell-O within seconds. He held her squirming little form, while Brooke gently swabbed her face and neck and arms. He glanced at Brooke's face. The tenderness in it made him look swiftly away.

But not before he felt the piercing awareness of the road he had not taken. He had missed all of this in his life by choosing career over family. For the first time, he understood what he had lost. And for the first time, he contemplated the crossroads he stood at. Could a man choose again?

Lexy crowed and bounced up and down on her seat. She laughed. Mostly she splashed. By the time they were done, the baby was dry and wrapped securely in a towel, while Cole and Brooke were soaked.

The wet shirt again. Lord have mercy.

"I'll get her dressed," he said gruffly. "While you go change."

Stupid to have volunteered. Stuffing the clean baby back into sleepers was nearly twice as tough as getting her out had been. Especially now that he'd dismissed his helper.

He had just done up the last snap, when he heard the front door open. He tucked the baby under his arm and went to see what surprise life had decided to deliver this time.

The first thing he saw was two large packages of diapers. Only after he had mentally greeted them with the enthusiasm one might normally reserve for the rescuing cavalry did he turn his attention to the women who had delivered them.

Two middle-aged women, loaded down with grocery bags, and bustling with energy and good cheer. Neither was a movie star.

They introduced themselves, Monique, the housekeeper, and Brenda, the nanny.

Brooke came down the stairs, looking better than ever in casual jeans and a white button-down shirt, rolled up at the sleeves. She obviously knew both the women and hugged them in greeting. She kissed the diaper packages!

"I can't believe you don't have power yet," Monique said. "The work crew on the road said the last pole went up yesterday."

Experimentally, she flicked the main hall-light switch and the chandelier above the stairs winked to life.

Cole could feel the color moving up his neck. Why hadn't he, disaster expert, tried the power first thing this morning? Instead, they had done everything the hard way.

And he was so glad. And he knew that's why he hadn't even tested the power. Because he didn't want it to be back on.

That was their excuse to be together. That was the glue. Once they had power—and all this help from town—Brooke wouldn't need him anymore. Their relationship, if it could be called that, was based on him rescuing and her needing to be rescued. With that gone, would anything remain? It seemed like an unlikely basis for a romance.

He, of all people, should know the intensity that came in these kinds of situations, the bonds that flourished and felt as if they would last forever but never did. One or two phone calls, a couple of exchanged letters, and it dwindled out.

Brooke didn't need him anymore.

His eyes sought hers above the children who had catapulted down the stairs and were dancing circles in the foyer in celebration of the return of electricity.

But Brooke looked as devastated by this new development as he felt.

The kids, however, did not share the sense of loss.

"I'm showering for an hour," Saffron screamed. "Then I'm blowing my hair dry. Then I'm using my curling iron."

"I get the Nintendo!" Calypso announced and headed for the stairs, talking to himself, "Double 07, then Mario, then...." His voice faded at the top of the stairs.

Darrance emerged from the shopping bags the housekeeper had brought with boxes stuffed under his arms. "I'm microwaving! Pizza Pockets, then Bagel Bites, then popcorn."

"TV work?" Kolina asked her nanny. "*101 Dalmatians?*"

"Let's get it warmed up in here, and then *101 Dalmatians* it is." She waltzed over to the thermostat on the wall, fiddled, and then he heard the fans whir to life. Within seconds steady puffs of warmth were coming out of the floor registers.

He watched as they each went their separate ways, these children who had become so important to him. Who had needed him. Now they didn't, either.

Suddenly, he and Brooke were alone in the foyer.

"I think I liked it better before," she said, voicing exactly what he was feeling.

"Come on," he said, not wanting to let his own sudden sense of loss show. "You're dying for a nice hot bath."

"Ha. It'll be hours before there's enough water for Saffron *and* everyone else."

"I've noticed this before," he said, gesturing at the empty foyer. "Electricity changes everything. If you go into a village with no power the families are all playing games together, at night the whole village gathers in the square for storytelling and plays. Once a society has electricity, everyone sits in their own houses and watches TV.''

''And plays Nintendo,'' she said softly.

''I mean, you can't go backward in time. I know that. Except for isolated moments.''

''I'm glad I got to be here for a few of those isolated moments,'' she said softly.

What was she saying? That she liked him? That maybe, even with the lights on, this thing that leaped in the air between them could be explored?

But he did not want to explore his own vulnerability right now. Instead, he did what he did best. He hid his feelings by taking action. Taking charge.

''Look, I'll get those mattresses back up the stairs, and then I'd like to run Granny into town and get her head checked. I'm sure it's fine, but a doctor should have a quick look at it.''

She nodded solemnly, understanding these were clean-up tasks, loose ends, before they said goodbye.

''I should go retrieve my car, too,'' she said, as good as him at using action to cover all those uncomfortable feelings. ''I'll help with the mattresses first.''

He wanted to tell her no, he didn't want her help, but somehow he could not manage a lie of that magnitude. He wanted to be with her, for just a little while longer.

She was hilarious on the other end of a mattress. Not very strong, but very determined. Somehow, with great huffing and puffing, they got the mattresses up the stairs and onto the right beds. Monique moved behind them, stripping sheets.

''Where are all the clean sheets? And I can't seem to find a single towel.'' The housekeeper gave them baffled looks when Brooke and Cole burst into laughter.

"I'll get some from the store in town when I take Granny," he said. "They won't be House of Bruce."

"Bryan," Brooke corrected him absently, and they both started laughing again.

They made their way back into the main living room. After all the activity, after it being such a hub over the last few days, the room looked strangely empty when restored to its normal dignity. Even Granny was missing.

He parted with Brooke and found Granny in her suite, an extra heater blaring away furiously at her feet as she sat glued to the television.

"I thought maybe you and I should take a run into the doctor," he said.

"It'll have to wait. I've already missed three days of my soaps. I am not missing another episode. Cassandra married Jake while I was gone, and Betty was found! She had amnesia from falling down the stairs after she overheard Blake and Vanessa talking about their affair. Three days! My gosh, a lot can happen in three days."

"You're not kidding," he said.

She gave him a shrewd look. "You know what I think?"

She was going to tell him what she thought, whether he wanted to hear or not. "You should spend the day with Brooke. She's a good girl, but way too serious and worn to a frazzle. Get her out of here for the day. Give her a break. Make her laugh, for God's sake."

He could feel himself starting to smile. Still needed after all. And making somebody laugh wasn't quite the same as romance, though he was sure he caught a little gleam in Granny's eye. Was the old gal matchmaking?

"Maybe I'll do that," he said, trying not to sound too excited about the idea. "But who's going to take you to the doctor?"

"Oh, Monique can do it. We can chat about the soaps all the way to town. And men. Maybe we'll chat about you."

He was actually going to blush. "About me?"

"You're kind of a handsome and intriguing devil. But don't get a swelled head over it." She waved him away and turned her attention back to her program.

He found Brooke in the kitchen unpacking groceries. Darrance was sitting at the table with a litter of boxes and wrappers around him, looking vaguely ill.

"Um," Cole said and suddenly felt like the schoolboy he had once been. Shy. Socially awkward. Different. "I can drive you up to your car after I get my driveway cleared."

That wasn't what he'd intended to say at all.

"Oh, that's not necessary. Monique and I can do it."

He studied his thumb, looked up, glanced away, "Granny suggested maybe you could use a break."

"Me?" Brooke said. He realized it might have sounded a little better if it was his idea rather than Granny's but he was new at this stuff. Was he asking her for a date? Wouldn't the two R's follow swiftly on the heels of a date?

"Yeah. You know. Because the kids were so rotten to you yesterday." That was so different and not nearly as scary as saying, I'd like to spend some more time with you.

The difference registered in her eyes. "Um."

He took a deep breath and committed himself to everything life was holding out to him. "I feel like I could use a break, too, some grown-up time."

"Really?" She sounded marginally more enthused, but she still wasn't making this easy for him. Was it possible she was as bad at this as he was?

"With you," he said gruffly.

And her smile was radiant.

"I have a boat," he hurried on. "I wondered if you might like to spend some time on the lake today? We'll catch some fish, have dinner at my place."

"I'll come fishing!" Darrance called.

"Not this time, buddy. What do you think, Brooke?"

"Yes," she said and then blushed at how quickly she had said yes. "I mean, I'll be terrible at fishing."

"That always makes the fish happy," he said and was rewarded with another smile. She was eager to spend time with him. Oh, hell. He was sure to disappoint. Why had he said fishing? He could take her for dinner in town. What else was there to do in town? Creston was a little farming town of seven thousand people. Pretty as a jewel, it still had nothing that would compare to what she would be used to in Los Angeles.

There was a bowling alley. "Would you rather go bowling?" Not that she looked like the bowling type.

"No!" she said. "Fishing sounds fine. Exciting. I've never done it before."

Fishing was relaxing. Contemplative. Exciting?

"Look, if you'd rather go out for dinner, there's a couple of decent places we could try." He was making this more like a date by the second.

"Actually, your first plan sounded terrific."

Oh, geez, now he had to produce terrific. No wonder he didn't do stuff like this more often. He contemplated killing Granny for putting this ridiculous notion in his head, but it was too late. Besides, the notion had already been in his head. Granny had just spurred him to action.

He looked at his watch. "Say, at two o'clock? I'll meet you here, and we can walk down to my dock."

"Oh, you don't have to meet me. I can find my way."

"I want to," he said and realized how true it was. He wanted to be with her. He wanted to walk the forest floor with her hand in his. He wanted her to see his world. Maybe asking her to go fishing had not been a mistake after all.

"All right," she said softly. "See you at two."

Now he'd gone and done it. He turned quickly away before he did the reasonable thing and changed his mind.

Cole Standen had asked her out. Okay, with a little prodding from Granny, but he had still asked her out. He hadn't even considered Darrance's request to go with them.

Could it really be that he wanted to spend time with her? Just her? After the terrible impression she'd made?

Brooke kept getting these chances to make another impression. To not take them would be like shaking a fist at the gods.

She liked him! Okay. More than liked him. She felt as if she were on fire when she was around him. She felt as if she couldn't breathe, and fully alive at the very same time. She felt as if life was full of the most amazing possibilities. What was so wrong with that? Wasn't it the most normal and natural thing in the world for a man and a woman to like each other, to feel that spark arcing in the air between them, to want to see where it led?

Okay, she had not done so well in this arena in the past.

But she had the oddest and nicest feeling of not having a past. Of having just been born, clean and new, as if life was full of fresh opportunities and chances.

"What do you wear fishing?" she asked, bursting into Granny's suite.

"The peach lounging outfit?" Granny suggested.

"Fishing! Not eating bonbons and playing footsie!"

"Shh. Betty's remembering the awful truth about Blake and Vanessa."

But Brooke did not want to be around people, even ones on television remembering awful truths. No, she wanted to live, just a while longer in the bubble of this brand-new world.

"I'll figure it out," she told Granny.

And she did. The jeans and the white shirt would be fine for fishing, but she'd need something warm on the water. Having gotten quite accustomed to raiding Shauna's closet, she helped herself to a suede sheepskin-lined jacket, a Calvin Klein. She pulled back her hair and popped on a Dodgers baseball cap and thought she looked perfect!

He wanted to be with her. She wanted to be with him! They were going out on his boat, together. What could be more perfect than that?

Three hours later she was puking her guts out over the side of his boat.

"Are you okay?" he called.

The chop had come up on the water out of nowhere. Until then it had been a serene day, the water still, mirroring the surrounding snowcapped mountains. They had laughed and chattered like the best of friends.

But then the wind stirred and picked up. Chop had progressed to swells. Now the boat was sliding in and out of three-foot troughs.

"Fine," she called bravely and debated going forward. He had cut the motor once to come back and check on her, but that had only made the boat toss more, like a cork in a bathtub. It also meant it would take longer to get back to solid ground. "Why didn't I pick bowling?" she wailed out loud.

It had started off so nicely, too. As it turned out, fishing required lots of close contact, while he showed her how to set the hook and cast the line. At one point his arms had been around her, guiding her through the motions.

It had all been perfect until the chop on the water. Her stomach had started to feel a touch squeamish.

But he had so obviously felt nothing, standing legs apart with his face into the wind, so at home on the water. She had thought she must be overreacting.

And then a fish had hit. It was when he had pulled it in, all slimy and bug-eyed and gasping desperately for air that she realized she wasn't just a touch squeamish. She was feeling quite a lot squeamish.

The next thing she knew, she had her head over the side of the boat, heaving until she thought she would turn inside out. She watched helplessly as Shauna's Dodgers hat, signed by someone famous, bobbed away.

His hand had been on her neck the whole time. He stroked and talked to her in a low, crooning tone.

"I'm so sorry," she said in between hurling. "I can't believe this."

"Why is it I have a feeling nothing with you is ever going to go quite as I plan it?" He didn't sound nearly as upset as she thought he could be. Sympathetic and faintly amused.

"Why?" Her stomach cleared briefly, and she sat on one of the leather benches that lined the deck. "What did you plan?"

"A scenic day on the water. I was going to find out everything there was to know about you. I was going to find out what you majored in at high school, what kind of flowers you like, where you grew up, how you ended up in a career in L.A.''

"Oh, well," she managed to say. "You aren't missing much." There was puke on the collar of Shauna's jacket. She closed her eyes and tried to take her mind off her stomach.

"That was just the warm-up." She sensed he was trying to keep her mind off her stomach, too, and the roiling in the water that her stomach was insisting on imitating. "Because I was also thinking of a little hand-holding and eye-gazing."

He put his arm around her shoulder, companionably, just as if she wasn't splattered in horrible substances and drenched in the sweat of one who planned on being very ill.

"Oh," she said, though it came out suspiciously sounding like a moan. Hand-holding. Eye-gazing. Be still, damn stomach.

"If the eye-gazing and hand-holding thing went okay, I might have tried to steal a kiss. Or two. Or three."

Kissing. Yes! Yes! Yes!

But her body said, no, no, no, and in no uncertain terms. He had barely gotten the word kiss out of his mouth when she pushed his arm off her shoulder and twisted violently to get her head back over the side.

She was mostly successful, though she knew Shauna's jacket was never going to be the same.

"Don't take it personally," she gasped. "It had nothing to do with you talking about kissing. Really."

"Believe me, kissing you has fled my mind. I have to get you to shore. And you know what? We're a long way out."

"How far?" she asked bleakly.

''I think we're an hour back to my place, if the water stays calm.''

If this was calm, she was in hell. She was in hell, anyway. The most gorgeous, sexy man on the planet had asked her to spend the afternoon with him. He obviously had a little romance on his mind. And this had to happen?

On the other hand, she had always been a perfectionist, the one who *made* things go her way and forced the world to fit her mold. She had *earned* the respect and caring of others.

But when he glanced back at her from the front of the boat, she saw something in the kindness of his eyes that she had not experienced before.

Whatever he felt for her, it was unconditional. It did not rely on her being perfect, on her performance.

With her head hanging over the side of the boat, it seemed to her she was set free, that she caught a glimpse of what love was.

It seemed like it was hours later that she felt the bump of the boat docking. From where she was lying, she watched blearily as he leaped from the deck to the dock and moored the boat safely.

He was back in a moment, crouched over her. One arm slid under her shoulders, the other under her knees.

She wanted to protest. But she had no strength left. The temptation of being looked after was just too great. So instead of resisting, she let herself relax into his glorious strength.

''I'm so sorry,'' she muttered again. ''Do I smell like puke? Say no, even if I do. Or I'll kill myself.''

''Hey, after three days of handling Code Brown, what's a little puke between friends?'' He adjusted her weight and took a step from the boat. She could feel it the moment the ground turned solid under his feet.

"Put me down so I can kiss the ground," she said.

"Let's delay the kissing till later."

"I hope that's going to be as good as it sounds."

He smiled. "I hope so, too. But you know what? I kind of doubt it."

She cuddled into the broadness of his chest, feeling it again, that sense of being cared about without having to earn it or perform for it. She was sick as a dog and happy as a lark. He strode along the forest path, and she took deep greedy breaths of earth air.

They came to his cabin. Compared to Shauna's house it wasn't grand, and yet Brooke was immediately taken with it.

Built of weathered gray logs, the windows were all French-paned glass, the lakeside was wall-to-wall windows that all opened onto a huge multilayered deck.

"Is that a hot tub?" she asked.

"Yeah. Electrically heated, unfortunately."

She said an unladylike word. He laughed.

He kicked open the door and set her on the couch and she looked around, faintly amazed by what a cozy space it was. A fire was going in a potbellied black stove in the corner of the living room, and the room was comfortably heated. Even though she shivered. He set her on the couch and looked down at her.

"You look good in green," he teased, unfolded a plaid blanket from beside the couch and tucked it carefully around her.

"I'm not wearing green, so I assume you mean my face."

"What can I get you to drink? I have a nice 1969

Alka-Seltzer Bordeaux, or a sparkling Alka-Seltzer Cooler. Your choice.''

"Oh, I'll live dangerously. Just bring me one of each.''

"You got it.'' He left, and she could hear him in his kitchen. She wished she could see him. He came back a moment later with a big crystal glass that fizzed and foamed.

She took a tentative sip, smiled. "Good year.''

"Thanks.''

Within a very short while, she was feeling much better—though not up to the fish he had planned for dinner.

They just sat on the sofa and talked. She felt as if she had known him forever. It seemed so surprising that he had to ask her about herself, when it seemed as though he should know all there was to know.

After a while she got up and wobbled off to the bathroom, cleaned herself up as best she could. He knocked on the door and handed her a T-shirt. She swilled his mouthwash and sponged the worst of the mess off Shauna's jacket.

Now, maybe they could get to the part they both had been waiting for since the moment they met.

Back on the couch, he took her hand in his. He ran his thumb down her wrist and up it, along the line of her arm, up the column of her throat.

He trailed that thumb over her lips, softly, and, impulsively, she kissed it.

His thumb stopped, and she kissed it again, feeling the texture of it, the hardness. She nipped it lightly, and he moved it to the back of her neck, pulling her head closer to his.

And then he kissed her. Not that gentle little brush of lips that had happened before. No, a real kiss.

After all that had happened, that kiss told her he still liked her, still wanted to move forward. She did not want to think right now about what forward meant.

She just wanted to melt into this moment. Everything else disappeared. Every single thing she had been before was gone.

His lips on hers, questing, demanding, healing, led her to who she was going to be. A woman bold and sensuous, sure of herself and her place in the world.

A woman loved.

He was both tender and savage. He was the storm and the calm. The darkest night and the first rays of dawn.

His kiss deepened, asking more of her, and she gave it willingly. He called to something in her that had not yet been born—the essence of who she was, a place so pure and so deep within her she had never explored those depths before.

She pulled his shirt from where it was tucked into the band of his jeans. She ran her hands possessively over the hard, flat line of his belly, up to the hard crest of his breastbone, across the mounds of his pecs. His skin felt like silk over steel. Her fingertips felt thirsty, as if they had wandered the desert and found an oasis.

From far, far away she heard a terrible jangling. She lifted her head, confused.

"It's just the phone. Repaired, as if I give a damn," he said. "Ignore it."

But it rang and rang and rang.

"What if it's the kids?" she asked finally, the ring grating on her nerves, spoiling what really should have been a perfect moment. "Why would they be so persistent if it wasn't an emergency?"

He said two words in a row that he must have learned

in the company of men. He made a grab for the phone and lifted the receiver.

"What?" he snapped. "Who?" He listened for a long time, not saying a word, his expression growing darker. "Yeah, I'll tell her."

He hung up the phone, folded his hands over his belly, and looked at the ceiling long and hard, as if he was trying to contain his temper.

"What?" she said, feeling the shift of emotion in the room.

"That was your boss. She's back."

"Oh."

"She's right here in Heartbreak Bay, so she could see the lights on down here. Couldn't figure out why we weren't answering the phone since it was so obvious we were home."

"Oh."

"It seems we've been summoned," he said darkly.

"Oh," Brooke said again, but what she really meant was *oh, no*.

Chapter Seven

Brooke simply did not feel ready for this. The test. They had barely started having fun! She felt terrible regret that so much of their day together had been spoiled.

But if she was unhappy about this development, it was obvious that he was unhappier. Cole glared at the ceiling, his eyebrows furrowed. She braced herself, in case he started cursing, but, finally, with nothing more than a sigh, he turned and looked at her.

He picked up her hand, lifted it to his mouth, and blew on her thumb. His breath was as warm and sensuous as a touch. That small gesture contained such promise, said so much about the kind of man he was and how he handled disappointment.

Brooke battled an impulse to pull the phone cord right out of the wall and return to the sweet savagery of his kiss. But thwart Shauna? If her summons was not answered, she would not hesitate to march right down here and hammer on the door.

"What kind of person," Cole growled, "knowing two

adults of mature age are in residence and not answering the phone, would persist?''

The kind who didn't want anything serious to occur until certain tests of character had been conducted and passed.

There was nothing wrong with Shauna's reasoning. ''Better to know now that he's a snake,'' she'd said of Brooke's ex-boyfriend Keith, ''than later. Nothing more embarrassing than finding him shedding his skin after something as irrevocable as 'I do' has happened.''

Somehow, Brooke knew Cole wasn't going to appreciate that under her cavalier manner, Shauna really did care about Brooke. She had the gut feeling Cole would be offended by the notion that her employer had better sense, better instincts than Brooke herself did.

Wasn't there something vaguely offensive about that assumption, now that she thought about it? Of course, there was her history to consider.

''She worries about me,'' Brooke said, a half explanation for Shauna's pushiness.

''She worries about you? Seriously? Like you're one of her children?''

''Something like that.'' She felt a need to defend her boss. ''You saw me left to my own devices. Explosions. Fire.'' Which would just about describe her relationship efforts, too. Disasters, each and every one.

He had no idea what her frame of reference was. ''That's not fair. You were totally out of your element. I imagine in your job you radiate competence. I bet you put out fires, not start them.''

''Thanks, I am very good at my job.'' She really did feel grateful to him for seeing that, given what a mess she had made of looking after the house and kids for a few hours on her own.

"Well, that being as it may, I think you should call her back. Tell her you're busy." He did that little thing with her thumb again and glanced up at her with mischief lighting his sapphire eyes.

Brooke actually managed a strangled little laugh. It would be like refusing a summons from the queen. "Uh," she said, trying to put it in a way that wouldn't present either her or Shauna in a horrible light, "I don't exactly have a nine-to-five job. Shauna calls. I go."

"What about your personal life?"

"Well, to be perfectly honest, I don't have one." And up until this point, because of the disasters, she had not really missed the fact.

"And what if you decided you wanted one?"

He'd have to pass the test first. The funny thing was that Brooke knew Shauna really did have her best interests at heart. What Shauna wanted for Brooke was exactly what Shauna had with Milton—honesty, friendship, communication, with a whole pile of passion thrown in for good measure.

"I guess if I decided I needed more personal time, I'd have to negotiate something with Shauna. Or look for a new job." If the beau didn't pass the test, and Brooke persisted in pursuing the relationship, she knew which of those it would be, too.

"Hmm. And I thought the military owned me. I can't decide if I'm happy or sad that your life is so pathetic."

"Hey! My life is not pathetic."

"Well, your personal one is. No, wait. Pathetic would be overstating something that is nonexistent."

He was teasing her, gently, but there was a bite behind the words, too. Probably because they were true.

"So, why would it make you happy if my life was pathetic?"

"No competition. No guys waiting in the wings. Nothing happening that is more exciting than me."

Whatever offense she had taken melted. "Are you planning to romance me, Major?"

"Oh, yeah," he said softly and nibbled at the inside of her wrist. His lips were warm and firm, and she felt shooting sensations all the way up to her shoulder.

She also felt gloriously happy. Her pathetic life suddenly filled with hope and promise. The sooner they got the test over with the better. Cole Standen was planning to romance *her*.

"What exactly does romance mean to you?" she whispered.

He nibbled some more, looked up at her through the thick fringe of his lashes. "Did you have to ask? I'm rusty in that department." He sighed. "Okay, you asked. Fishing is out, I guess. So how do you feel about bowling?"

"Do you have to put your arms around me to show me how?"

"I think so."

"I like bowling, then."

"Did you just want to skip ahead to the arms-around-you part?"

She nodded, then realized she was being led astray. Before the test. There would be plenty of time for bowling, or substitutes, after. If he passed. She pulled reluctantly away from the lips that had made it past her wrist and were now nuzzling the soft flesh of her inner arm.

"Call her back," he suggested again.

"I can't," she wailed and leaped to her feet before he made her completely lose her senses. Shauna said a girl needed to keep her senses at times like these, not lose them.

"Why not?" He gazed at her lazily, winked.

Winked! Was there anything sexier than a man giving that intimate wink, as if he knew all kinds of secrets and planned to let you in on them all?

"It's not the nature of my job," she said out loud. Inwardly, she pleaded for the strength to keep her senses. "Shauna can be demanding, but I get paid a king's ransom to make sure her demands are fulfilled."

"Is that why you work for her? The money?"

"Well, it's part of it. But part of it is the excitement, too."

"Ah. Makes up for the lack of excitement in your personal life." He got to his feet, came too close. "We can change that," he promised.

"Bowling?" she challenged him, backing away.

"The part that comes after bowling." He came one step forward for her every one step back, until she felt the wall against her back.

A shiver went up and down her spine. She had the feeling the kind of excitement he offered would make the thing she had called excitement in the past a tawdry thing.

"You don't have to come back with me to the house," Brooke said. She shoved off from the wall, ducked under his arm and headed for the door. "Maybe that would be better."

Much better. The test could wait until another day. Another month. Another year. Maybe he didn't even have to take the test. Wouldn't it be better to always just wonder, to cherish her memories, than to *know?*

She tucked in her shirt, wiped her mouth. She looked sadly at the jacket before she put it back on.

"Oh, I'm coming," he said. "I wouldn't miss this for the world."

"That's what I was afraid of."

"I'm not sending you back to explain about the towels all by yourself."

"And the sheets," she reminded him sadly. "And the rug." And the jacket. Of course, these were probably the least of their problems now, but there was no sense warning him. What good was a test, if a person had been warned? That would be like cheating.

Still, she took comfort in the look on his face, fiercely protective of her. His hand in hers as they followed the moonlight-illuminated path back around the lake also gave comfort. It was so strong, so sure. Real.

Trust him, her heart begged her.

"I'm sorry it has to end like this," Brooke said, stopping in the shadow of the trees as they approached the house.

"End? Is it over?"

"Well, today is. And you're probably thinking, thank God. I've been a fiasco, haven't I?"

"I wouldn't have put it that way, no."

"Well, how would you have put it? I got seasick on your boat. I couldn't eat dinner. And then my boss called."

"I guess I'd put it that life is always full of surprises. Most of the time that's a good thing."

"It is?" she whispered.

"See? The moonlight turns your hair to silver, and your eyes to indigo pools. That's a nice surprise."

She noticed how the moonlight etched his own features and made him look strong and sure, a man who could surely pass any test the world threw at him.

He leaned toward her, took her lips again. And her lips answered him with who she really was. The kiss deepened. She could feel what was real in her bursting to get out.

She could feel her wildness and her glory, her fullness as a woman. He tangled his hands in her hair, and he savaged her mouth, making her respond to him.

She changed her mind. They were going back to the cabin and locking the door against the world, against tests, against every reality but this one. This one was how very right his lips felt on hers.

And then the front door swung open, and they were illuminated in a band of light.

"Yoo-hoo? Are you out there?"

He swore under his breath. Brooke pulled away from him. He turned and squinted at the doorway.

"What is wrong with her?" he snapped after he said a few more choice words.

She's on a mission to save me from myself. Sorry.

"I'm sure she's just eager to meet you, Cole."

"I think she could have the good manners to wait until after I'm done kissing you," he muttered.

"Waiting is not one of Shauna's strong suits."

"Really? What are her strong suits, then?"

Oh, boy, you are about to find that out.

Cole turned and faced the woman on the step. She was dramatically shielding her eyes, squinting into the darkness.

Her strong suit was obvious. Even from a distance, she was a stunning figure, beautiful and perfect like a porcelain doll. She was wearing some kind of flowing peach-colored pajamas that were utterly ridiculous and yet suited her. The filmy fabric floated around her, accentuating her every feature. Long straight black hair,

like Saffron's, fell in wild, but somehow contrived, disarray around her shoulders.

As he and Brooke moved closer, he remembered her
face. Amazing. Huge blue eyes contrasting with that
black mane of hair, faintly copper-colored skin, a figure
that seemed like a biological impossibility. How could
someone with such large breasts have such a tiny waist?

He remembered he had debated that last year, too,
right before he threw her bikini-clad body right off his
beach.

He remembered, too, thinking then exactly what he
thought now. That there was something about her perfection that was faintly plastic. Her face didn't have a
wrinkle on it, but she had a daughter nearly twelve?

The miracles of Botox, he thought cynically.

"There you are," she gushed as Brooke came up the
stairs, into the circle of light. He held back, watching
her take both Brooke's hands and peck her cheeks as if
they were long-lost relatives. "My, you're all flushed."

This statement was loaded with interest, as if she
wanted a complete rundown, but she didn't wait to get
it. She let go of Brooke's hands and then stepped back.
She gazed at her assistant appraisingly, a feline smile on
her lips. God, the woman knew Brooke had just had the
daylights kissed out of her.

And then her eyes narrowed and she frowned, ever so
faintly. "That isn't my jacket, is it?"

"Well, yes, it is, but—"

Brooke's boss remembered him and said breezily, he
guessed for his benefit, "Oh, it's all right. We'll talk
about that stuff later."

With a big deduction to the paycheck, he guessed.
Would he have been burning towels so happily if he'd
thought Brooke might have to pay for them?

Shauna turned slowly to him, motioned to him to come out of the darkness. When he did, she eyed him with frank and undisguised appreciation. She widened her eyes and smiled. Sensuously? That had to be his imagination.

"And you must be Major Standen," she exclaimed huskily, coming down the stairs toward him. "The children and my mother have talked of nothing else. My, my, can't I see why?"

This wasn't how she'd reacted to him on his beach last summer. Oh, no, then he'd been treated like the local yokel who should have been thrilled by a visit from royalty.

Now, he felt as if he was being inspected like a side of beef. He stepped back before she could buss him on both cheeks. Lady, he wanted to say, this ain't Hollywood. Instead, he sent Brooke a look, hoping for rescue, but she was scraping at a spot on the jacket with her fingernail.

"Come in," Shauna said, missing the signal that he didn't like physical familiarity from strangers. She looped her arm though his. He didn't really want her arm through his, but for Brooke's sake he was going to try, for once in his life, to be civilized.

So he didn't shake free of her, and he pretended to listen to her endless chatter. Every single word out of her mouth was dramatic, as if she was always looking for her Academy Award. He was exhausted already.

He paused at the front door. "I just wanted to see Brooke home. I won't come in tonight."

The beautiful face collapsed into a pout that he recalled seeing on his beach last summer. "But the children want to see you! And, of course, I want to thank you for all you've done."

He shot Brooke a look asking her to extricate him from this, but she was still involved with the jacket. He sighed, straightened his shoulders and trailed after the actress into her now-familiar house.

The children were on him in a heartbeat, squealing and hugging and all talking at once. Cole was removed from his discomfort temporarily and hugged each of his little darlings with all his heart. Shauna was looking at him, something he couldn't read in her face.

Cynicism? Not quite. No, more like a desire to believe in something, overlaid with the hardness of one who did not believe in much. But why would such a look be directed at him?

He was introduced to Milton and remembered him from the beach, too. Remembered him only in that he was so forgettable, totally eclipsed by the beauty of his wife. Milton seemed like the least likely match for the actress—even his skin seemed rumpled, like Einstein in a younger body. But his handshake was firm, and his quiet thanks to Cole heartfelt.

And then the children were whisked away by a nanny, and Cole found himself sitting in the living room that had been his home for days.

"Drink?" Shauna asked.

"No, thanks."

"You look like a Scotch man," she said, pouring him one, anyway, which gave her an excuse to waltz over with it and sit next to him on the couch. Too close.

He hated Scotch. Wishing he'd chosen a chair, he sidled away from her and looked around the room. He decided he hated the living room like this. Perfect. Everything in its place. No mattresses, no dishes, no fire in the hearth. It had become a formal and cold room.

It had been such a lively place. Shauna was moving

into his space again. She was so beautiful. Why did she remind him of a barracuda?

"So, Major," Shauna said breathily, "I want to know all about *you*." She rested her hand on his forearm, then slid her hand up and down his arm, and gave his muscle the tiniest squeeze.

He cast a look at Milton, hoping he'd get up and give him a punch in the nose, but Milton was looking dreamily out the window over the black waters of the lake. Brooke was sitting in a chair in the corner, her shoulders hunched, looking for all the world as if she was going to cry.

Probably about that damn jacket. Or the towels.

He brushed Shauna's hand off his arm and, forgetting his hatred for Scotch, swallowed his drink in a single gulp. He glanced at Brooke through watering eyes.

She looked worse than she had with her head hanging over the side of his boat! Her face was white and pasty. She looked as if she was going to throw up again.

For God's sake, he didn't care what her employer wanted, or why she'd been summoned back so urgently.

"About you?" Shauna reminded him, her hand back on his arm.

Enough was enough. He was done being civilized. He looked pointedly at her hand, until, faintly flustered, she removed it.

"I don't think right now is a real good time to get to know each other." *Never* sounded like a good time. "Brooke hasn't been feeling well. I think we should let her go to bed and call it a night."

"Brooke hasn't been well?" Shauna shot her assistant a look, seemed to notice her for the first time, and notice how ill she looked. "But darling," she pouted, "I need you to go to L.A. tomorrow for me!"

"I'll be fine by tomorrow," Brooke said through tight lips.

"I hope so," Shauna said. "My life is a disaster. I am amazed by what you do for me. Getting by without you has been a nightmare." She shuddered delicately.

But Cole could feel a cold rage beginning to burn inside him. Brooke was sick, and all her self-centered boss could see was how she would be affected by it? He had to get out of here before he did something Brooke might not like.

Tomorrow? He didn't want her going anywhere tomorrow. He was just beginning this business of getting to know her.

"I think whether Brooke travels or not tomorrow will depend on how she feels," he said stiffly.

"My, aren't we masterful," Shauna said silkily.

The woman hurt his head.

"I have to go," he said. *Before I tell you what a bitch you are.*

"But I so wanted to get to know you better!"

"Life is full of disappointments," he said, uncomfortably aware of how both Milton and Brooke were watching him as if he were center stage of some production.

"Tell you what! Major, why don't you join us for brunch in the morning? Around ten? I'd like to show you my appreciation for all you've done."

That probably meant she hadn't noticed her precious towels yet.

"You won't regret having come to my rescue."

If it had been her rescue, he figured he would have regretted it. But it had been her children, and he didn't regret that.

How did someone so crass, so superficial, have such nice kids? And nice employees? And a nice mom?

Oh, well, if she wanted to make the big gesture, that might be good. "Actually," he said, "I have something in mind. In terms of a reward."

She smiled, showing small white teeth that looked distinctly predatory. Brooke gave a tiny sound like a moan, and he glanced over at her.

She really wasn't looking well, as if she might have to bolt at any second.

So they could discuss the reward at brunch. He'd decided he was bargaining for the towels and sheets and that jacket.

He shot Brooke a look. Would she still be here at brunch? If she wouldn't be, he needed to talk to her. To find out when she would be back, when he was going to see her again.

"Brooke," he said, "do you want to see me out?"

"Oh, the poor darling looks so done in," Shauna said. "I'll see you out."

Her hand looped in his, and he had to shake her free again. The last thing he needed was to be "seen out" by another man's wife who didn't know how to keep her hands to herself. He stood up quickly. "I'll just see myself out. And see you at brunch tomorrow. Brooke, you'll still be here?"

She nodded miserably. She was about the same shade of green she had been after she'd left everything she'd eaten for the last week on the bottom of Kootenay Lake.

"Brooke, straight to bed," he said, and then turned on Shauna. "You don't ask one thing of her tonight."

"We just need to go over a few things, and then—"

He cut Shauna off. "Not one thing. Not one. Do you understand me?"

Milton was smiling absently, and then Shauna smiled, the first genuine expression he'd seen on her face. She could be beautiful, he thought, if she'd just get real. Brooke should give her a few lessons.

"Yes, Major," she said sweetly. "I do understand you."

"Good," he snapped and couldn't get out of that room fast enough.

In the morning, he was back, but he was prepared for what he was up against this time. He had his plan— negotiate his *reward* privately so that Brooke wouldn't know the exact terms, find a moment to talk to Brooke about what her plans were and when she would be back, and get away from Shauna as quickly as possible.

But of course the kids swarmed him as soon as he went in the door, Granny had to update him on Vanessa and Blake from the soaps, and Shauna glued herself to his side, a fact that did not seem to bother Milton in the least.

The only one he didn't really see was Brooke. She waved distractedly at him when he first came in, a cordless phone tucked by her ear and a sheaf of papers at her fingertips. She looked pale and out of sorts. He was willing to bet she'd got quite an earful about the jacket.

"Is she ordering towels?" he asked Shauna grimly.

She gave him a surprised look. "Now how on earth would you know that?"

"Just a guess."

Brooke joined them for brunch, an opulent affair with bowls overflowing with fresh fruit and platters of French toast and cinnamon rolls.

He sat next to her. "Hey. Say good-morning. Breathe."

She gave him a small pained smile that made him frown.

"Are you catching flak about those towels?" he said.

"I just have a ton of things to catch up on."

But she seemed distant, as if she deliberately was not engaging with him. What was going on here? She probably *had* caught flak over the towels and sheets. She probably blamed him, somewhat.

He took her hand under the table and squeezed it, an everything-is-going-to-be-fine gesture. And for a moment, she did connect, her eyes wide on his, searching his face, looking for an answer, but he did not know the question.

"Are you going today?" he asked.

"Yes. My flight's at three."

"And when will you be back?"

Again that look that begged him to answer a question he did not understand.

"I don't know."

"Brooke, is something wrong?"

"No." But she answered too quickly.

"It's those damn towels, isn't it? And the sheets? Is she giving you a hard time?"

"It hasn't been fun," she admitted, but he felt she was holding something back. Not telling him the full truth about the hell her employer was putting her through.

He scowled and realized it was time to make his move. He set down his napkin. "Shauna, I need to talk to you. In private."

Shauna shot her assistant a look that seemed vaguely concerned before that expression was wiped away with a more practiced look of contrived delight.

"Are we going to discuss your reward?" she purred.

"We sure as hell are."

"Anything you want," she said, rising from the table. Did she actually twitch her hips suggestively? He glared at Milton, who had a big bowl of porridge in front of him and apparently found that more interesting than his wife's shenanigans.

Brooke was looking at her own fruit-filled bowl with a fixed gaze.

"Milton," he said, "you'd better come, too."

"Oh, my, what do you want? Our house?" Shauna said with a giggle.

What he wanted was supervision!

Behind the closed office door, he took full responsibility for all the damaged items in the house and then laid out his terms.

Shauna sank back in a chair and stared at him, open-mouthed. "Are you telling me you thought I'd make Brooke pay for that stuff?" she finally asked.

"Or make her life miserable about it."

"You have the wrong impression of me," Shauna said, miffed.

But Milton laughed. "Don't worry. Her mother would never allow her to make Brooke pay for that stuff. And you know what? It is just stuff. We both are so grateful to you for stepping in and looking after things. Neither of us was particularly worried about the towels and sheets, nor the rug. I didn't like that rug, anyway."

"He didn't like the table you cut the legs off of, either," Shauna said. "Imagine, my baby having a Louis the Fourteenth changing table." She laughed, and her laughter was pealing and genuine.

Cole stared at her. The woman was a complete chameleon. He couldn't figure out, for the life of him, what she was really about.

"Just for the record," she said, "I asked Brooke to reorder linens, but I wasn't upset about it."

So that begged the question, what was Brooke so upset about this morning?

"What about the jacket?" he asked.

"Well," she admitted, "that is a different story. I mean, it was one of my favorite jackets and—Major, don't scowl at me like that! You asked. I'm telling you."

"Okay. That's what I want, then. For the reward. The jacket."

Her mouth fell open. "You're kidding, right?"

"Never been more serious in my life."

She studied him for a long time. "It's yours," she said softly. He wasn't sure what was going on, but she looked as if she was going to cry.

But she gave herself a shake, and the harder look reappeared on her face. "Now, Brooke mentioned to me you thought I should have better security. I'd like you to think about accepting the job."

"No."

"You haven't even heard my terms, yet." She named a figure that was astronomical.

"No," he said again, sharply. "I can put you in touch with someone. That's all." If it wasn't the damn linen bothering Brooke, what was it? He had a sudden, urgent need to talk to her, and he made his excuses and left the room.

But Milton's voice drifted out the open door. "I told you he was more man than you knew how to handle."

What kind of games did these people play?

And she responded, "I'm not done yet."

Oh, yes, she was, Cole thought with a shake of his head.

He went to find Brooke. It was Saffron who told him

Brooke had just left for the airport. He stood in the foyer, feeling stunned. She hadn't waited to say goodbye? She hadn't left a phone number?

What was going on in this weird house? He decided he wasn't waiting to find out. With his head hurting and his heart spinning, he marched out the door and back to his life.

Chapter Eight

Cole maneuvered his boat into the slip at his dock. The lake had really been too rough to go out on today. But maybe he had something in common with that long-ago young man who had walked these shores in his buckskins, with the wild wind lifting his long hair off his shoulders.

When he was hurt, Cole challenged himself, pushed himself, engaged in activity that required one hundred percent focus, did everything in his power to push away the pain.

And Cole was hurting. It had been three days since Brooke had left without saying goodbye. He kept expecting his phone to ring, and for it to be her.

But so far, it had not been, though his phone, usually so silent, rang often now. Saffron checking in, Darrance calling to ask a question, Calypso saying hi. Even Kolina seemed well versed in how to use the telephone.

A three-year-old could call him, but Brooke couldn't? Shauna had also been on the phone several times, always holding out some plum to him. The security job had been offered again, with more perks than his coffeemaker. He'd firmly given her the number of an old military friend, also retired, who might be interested.

Then she had called wondering if he would like to run fishing excursions on the lake for her when her friends came for visits. "Since Brooke had such a good time," she gushed.

Since Brooke apparently hadn't, Cole filled Shauna in on the exact details of what Brooke's good time on the lake had involved. That had been the end of that offer.

But she'd been back. Landscaping. Housepainting. She seemed certain that he needed a job that paid extravagantly. He'd been curt to the point of rudeness, but he couldn't help himself.

The film star made him uneasy. He was certain she had some hidden agenda that she was going to spring on him the instant he was foolish enough to tangle his life with hers. Last time she had called she had thought he might like to give swimming lessons to the kids when the seasons changed.

It was the only one of her offers that had tempted him, and only because he missed those kids more than he cared to admit. Plus, they lived close to water, a pool and a lake. They had to know how to swim, but he figured Shauna's latest offer might be moving her a step closer to his beach. He'd given her another name.

"Yoo-hoo."

He felt the hair on the back of his neck stand up. He straightened from where he was fastening his boat and turned.

Who else would call out that greeting? Here came Shauna, picking her way over the uneven ground on ridiculous heels, sashaying her hips. She was wearing some kind of swirling white beaded affair that might have been appropriate at the Oscars. But on the shores of Kootenay Lake? To his immense relief, he saw Saffron and Darrance were with her, which he hoped meant he wasn't going to have to fight her off with a stick.

She was clutching a large flat box. She tottered out on the dock, which was swaying in the rough water.

He had the uncharitable thought that if she fell in, he wasn't going in after her.

When had he become the kind of man who would watch a woman drown in front of her children? he wondered. The answer came swiftly. His heart had been hardening steadily with each passing day that he didn't hear from Brooke.

"Hi, kids." He hugged them both, then herded them off the dock before their mother fell in and he had to test his character.

He heard Saffron's complaints about how life was no more fun with the electricity back on, and he listened without offering an opinion to Darrance's arguments for a puppy.

As soon as it was marginally polite, he turned to Shauna. "What can I do for you?"

"Oh, no," she said, wagging a finger at him as if he had been a very bad boy. "It's what I can do for you."

"That's what I was afraid of," he muttered.

She held out the box. "Here's the jacket. I had it cleaned."

"Thanks." He took it reluctantly. The jacket was just a reminder that he had obviously felt stronger things for Brooke than she had felt for him.

In fact, last night, before sleep, he had entertained the very foolish notion that he might be in love with her.

Why else did she haunt him? Why did he think of her

lips and her eyes and the way her hair had felt slipping through his fingers? Why else would he plan so carefully what he was going to say to her next? What the next step in romancing her was?

Ha. Some romance. He'd been left at the starting gate.

Don't ask, he ordered himself, but of course, he asked. "How's Brooke?"

"Frantically busy. I have a film premiering at the end of the month, and there's so much work involved. We'll be having a party after, of course."

"Of course," he said dryly.

"Major, I have a teensy favor to ask you."

How had he known this was coming? He folded his arms over his chest, planted his legs wide and squinted narrowly at her.

Most people would have gotten the hint, would have been at least slightly intimidated by the stance, but then most people simply were not Shauna Carrier.

"I've been given an opportunity to work on a most amazing movie. About a military woman who becomes a prisoner of war."

"And you would be playing the part of?"

"The POW, of course."

He didn't know who had cast that one, but he really couldn't imagine a worse choice for the part than her. Miss Glamour-Puss in the military?

"It's based on a true story, and it's called *Spring in the Desert*. Do you get the double meaning? Like spring as the season or spring as the water."

He wished she would just quit babbling and get to the point.

Which she did, suddenly, catching him up the side of the head with it. "The thing is, this movie could be really important. A different kind of movie than what I usually make. It could have a very important message. This woman found hope and strength within herself under those terrible conditions.''

A novel concept to Shauna, he was sure, that hope and strength came from within and not from a movie contract or a big house on the hill.

''And this has what to do with me?'' he said, not even able to contain his impatience.

''I'm a little troubled by some of the technical aspects. They aren't ringing true with me. And if they aren't true to me, who is going to believe them?''

Who cares? But he found he did, a tiny bit. ''Look, uh, Shauna, that kind of subject material is really delicate to work with. It's the worst fear of anyone in the military. You can't trivialize it.''

''Exactly!'' she said. ''That's why I was wondering if I could get you to just take a look at some of the technical aspects for me. I've already told the producer that would be a condition of my taking the part. Having my own technical adviser.''

He gave her the short answer. ''No.''

There was that hand on his arm again. She batted her eyes at him. ''Please? It would be worth your while. You could be set for life.''

''What makes you think I'm not set for life now?''

''Brooke would like you to do it.''

''She would?''

Shauna nodded vigorously. ''She's going to be tied up in L.A. for a while. You could join her there.''

He wanted to romance Brooke here, on the quiet shores of this lake, following the footsteps of Eileen and Jimmy. He wanted to try calling birds from trees for her, and he wanted to walk the forest floor with her hand in his. He wanted to be sitting on that rock over there, with his arms wrapped around her, watching the sun go down.

He couldn't even imagine romance in a place like L.A. He'd been through there several times and it struck him as fast, flashy and noisy.

On the other hand there was probably more to do there than bowling.

And maybe if he really cared about Brooke—okay, loved her—it didn't have to be his way all the time. Maybe he had to give a little ground to the other party. An interesting concept for a military man. Giving ground was not in his vocabulary.

But that vocabulary did seem to be expanding. It now contained the word *surrender,* too. What if he just surrendered?

His pride was telling him to stay right here and wait for Brooke to give in and come back to him.

But his heart was whispering, *go.*

"I'll make it worth your while," she repeated, as if she sensed him weakening. She named a figure that was obscene.

"Whatever," he said. He tucked the box with the used jacket under his arm. It felt like the only currency he was going to need.

"Cole is coming to L.A.?" Brooke said into the phone. Her heart leaped foolishly. How she wanted to see him. How she had wanted, with every fiber of her being, to call him, to hear his voice, to laugh with him.

But everything was on hold, until he passed the test. Daily communication with Shauna had led her to believe he was going to pass.

But now this. Did the fact that Cole was coming to L.A. mean Shauna had finally found the right combination to make a man of such honor prostitute himself? He didn't seem like the type who would choose California for a holiday. No, he would more likely choose some high, windy and lonely mountain somewhere.

"In what capacity is he coming to L.A.?" she asked Shauna, and her heart fell when she got the answer. "A technical adviser on a film?"

There went any romantic notion she was entertaining that maybe he wanted to see her as badly as she wanted to see him.

God, she had done a stupid, stupid thing. She had fallen in love with that man. Head over heels. She should have waited until after the test.

But then this is what she was finding out; love didn't wait. It didn't obey the rules. It refused to be tamed or shoved into little boxes.

Because even though he was coming as a technical adviser and had succumbed to Shauna's latest attempt to buy him, Brooke felt as if she loved him still. Longed for him. Longed for his world of simplicity and forests and fires burning in hearths.

She could not imagine what had enticed him to come to her world. Money, she supposed, and lots of it. Perhaps no one was immune to opportunity shoved in their faces, perhaps no one could totally pass up the benefits of rubbing shoulders with someone famous.

"What, Shauna?" She couldn't believe she had heard that correctly. "You want me to pick him up at the airport, chauffeur him around? But usually part of the deal is that they stay away from me. Not this time? But why?"

Because Milton had told Shauna she might be risking life and limb to put such a demand on a man like Major Cole Standen.

"Are you saying you think he has feelings for me?" Brooke demanded. "Real feelings?"

And then her boss said the strangest thing. She said, "Brooke, no one else can tell you that. You have to trust yourself."

Trust herself. Brooke had known all along that was the lesson, but she was scared. She looked at the clock and felt her heart begin to hammer. Cole was going to be here, in her world, in less than twelve hours.

Soon, she would know the truth.

He seemed larger than life when he came through the international-flight gate at LAX several hours later. Brooke watched him with the advantage that he had not yet seen her, and her breath faltered at how extraordinary he was.

He was bigger than the average man, and, even in his casual suit, it was evident that frame was all hard muscle. People looked at him. Especially women, but his attraction was more than that.

He was more handsome than the average man, too, with that dark crisp hair and the vividness of those blue eyes. But that wasn't it either.

The mystery of his attraction was deeper. The way he carried himself with a certain unconscious grace and power that told the world who he was. The way his eyes swept the room. The line of his mouth.

Real.

But was he really?

She wanted to run to him, to fling her arms around him, to take his lips with hers, and let the kiss transport them back to a time before tests. A time of discovery and exploration. A time when she had felt, for a brief and beautiful moment, what it was to be a woman in love.

In love. Now, there was an emotion that could cloud all reason. How was she supposed to trust herself under these conditions?

So, flinging herself at him was out of the question since she had no idea what his motivation was in being here. It wasn't to see her, she reminded herself, he was following some carrot Shauna had held out for him.

But Shauna had not been full of her normal warnings. Their conversation had been absent of her cynicism and judgments.

Trust yourself, she had said to Brooke.

Well, trusting herself certainly did not mean obeying the impulsive, nearly delirious little voice inside her that just wanted to throw herself at him.

No, to earn her own trust she had to make measured judgments, rational judgments, judgments based on fact, not on emotion or wishful thinking or reading things that probably weren't there.

For instance, did his whole expression change when he saw her? Didn't it momentarily melt into gentle greeting, that firm mouth quirking upward in an irresistible smile?

No, she was sure it had not. A trick of her imagination, a trick of a mind seeing exactly what it wanted to see.

"Hello," she greeted him coolly. "Luggage?"

Again, she wondered if she was seeing just what she wanted to see. Was that disappointment that chased across his rugged features?

"So," she said brightly, when they were in her car and pushing their way through L.A. traffic. "What reward did you get from Shauna? I never did find out."

There, she thought proudly. Now she was being rational, cutting right to the chase.

He smiled. "I'm not telling."

All right, he was blocking. She tried a different tactic. "And she's hired you as a technical adviser on *Spring in the Desert?*"

"Free trip to California," he said with a careless shrug. "I love it already. Smell that air."

She knew a place in Santa Monica where the air was sweet and swept clean by the ocean breezes. She could kidnap him and take him there, instead of to the appointment at the studio.

"Do you want to go right to the studio?" she asked.

"What do you want to do?" he countered.

Kidnapping him and taking him to the beach was not rational thinking, she berated herself. Instead, she tried to harden herself to his presence in the vehicle. It was tough. He smelled so good she wanted to bury her nose in his neck at every traffic stop.

A bit desperately, she pointed out some of the attractions they were passing. She dared to slide a glance at his face when she used her pass to clear the gate at the front of the studio.

If he was impressed, he didn't show it.

She dropped him at the right office.

"Are we going to have some time together?" he asked before he shut the door.

"Oh, sure. I've been placed at your disposal for your entire visit."

"Have I done something wrong, Brooke? You don't seem yourself."

"Which self would that be? The one who demolishes barbecues or the one who heaves over the side of boats?"

He regarded her so steadily, she had to look away. "I'll see you later," she said. "Call my cell when you're done."

It was nearly eleven o'clock at night when she picked him up. His face was like thunder when he got in the car.

She drove him to Shauna's Hollywood Hills home, where a bedroom had been prepared for him.

"And use of the office," she said, showing him around. "If that's all, it's been a long, long day."

He took her elbow. "I'm done playing around," he said. "Come sit down and have a drink with me before you go. We need to talk."

"About?"

"About you and I," he said.

She gulped. But how could they ever be a couple if he was susceptible to Shauna's manipulations? Trust yourself, Shauna had said.

She looked into his eyes. They were tired, and his expression was worn. All she wanted to do was hold him, kiss the weariness from him.

She tried to think straight.

"If I stay, I want to know what the reward was," she said.

"Okay," he said with such boyish charm she knew she was lost.

A little while later they sat on the deck beside the pool. A little straw hut housed the cabana, and torches reflected in the water.

"You can't see the stars," he said, leaning his head back against his lawn chair.

"No, you can't."

"Don't you miss them?"

A man who had the wealth and pomp of the movie industry laid at his feet today, and he missed a sky with stars.

"Yes, I miss them," she said softly. She missed him. Being here with him made her so aware of the giant hole that had been opening in her soul since she left him.

She was supposed to be ferreting out his mercenary side, and she was allowing herself to be charmed instead.

"So how did you like the team at the studio?"

"I don't want to talk about it. I want to talk about this."

He passed her a big square flat box that he'd had behind the lawn chair. "This was the reward I asked Shauna for," he said.

She tried to guess what might be in it. Too light for a television or stereo. What had he asked for?

"Open it," he commanded softly.

Brooke opened the box, and shook out Shauna's suede, sheepskin-lined Calvin Klein jacket.

"For you."

"This is what you asked her for?" Brooke said, astounded. The tears clogged her eyes and throat instantly. She held the jacket into her face, hugged it. "But why?"

"I could tell she was going to be a real dog about it."

He was a great judge of character, because that was true. Brooke had figured, from the look on Shauna's face when she'd recognized her coat on Brooke, that she'd be paying for this jacket, one way or another, for a long, long time to come. "You could have had anything! A Ferrari probably!"

"Would a Ferrari have got me the look on your face right now?"

"The look on my face?"

"All soft and sweet and choked up, like you're going to cry. Not at all like the remote woman who picked me up at the airport."

"And that's worth more to you than a Ferrari? A woman with her makeup running and her nose threatening to?"

"I don't want a Ferrari, Brooke. I'm not that kind of man. And I guess I'm not the kind of man suited to consulting work either. No one really wanted to hear my opinions. They want to make one more movie that's full of romance and lies about the reality of war, and I'm not going to be able to stop them.

"And if I can't stop them, I'm sure as hell not going to help them. I'm going to go home. I don't belong here."

"So you aren't going to take the job from Shauna?" The warmth that had begun in the region of her heart when she opened the box grew.

"I kind of knew I wasn't cut out for movie work, Brooke. I guess I was looking for an excuse to come and see you."

"Me?" she whispered.

"I'm in love with you, Brooke."

He said the words so simply. Not decorated, not embellished. And yet his voice held the firmness of a man capable only of truth.

"You passed," she whispered through tears. And then she threw down the jacket and cast herself into his arms. "You passed," she cried. She covered him in kisses.

A long time later they came up for air.

"I don't get it," he said. "What do you mean, I passed?"

Laughing, she told him about the Shauna test, and its two parts. "First, she flirts with you, and then if you make it past that one, she offers you some wonderful temptation, a benefit to being close to her.''

She noticed he had gone very still. He put her off his lap, stood up and walked restlessly to the edge of the pool.

He glanced back at her. ''You're serious, aren't you?''

''About?'' she said, confused by his sudden withdrawal.

''You allowed her to subject me to some test? To play with me?''

''Well, it's not like that. She was protecting me.''

''Are you trying to tell me you couldn't tell who I really was? That after the time we spent together, so intensely, after you saw me changing Code Browns and cooking biscuits and telling stories by the fire, you're telling me you didn't know who I really was?''

She said nothing, seeing a terrible truth about herself, and feeling the greatest moment of her life slipping away.

Because she had not been brave enough to follow her heart, to obey it, to trust it.

He went on, the very lack of emotion in his voice causing her more fear than if he had yelled. ''You're telling me you trust your employer's judgment more than your own? Given who your employer is, I find that downright scary.''

''Cole—''

He held up his hand. ''Brooke, I've heard more double-talk than I can stand for one day. And you know what? All this time, I completely trusted who you were. I thought I saw underneath everything else. I thought I saw your soul. And now I think I've made a mistake.''

''No, you haven't,'' she said, choked. ''Cole, you saw who I was even when I lost sight of that myself.''

He took a deep breath, looked up again, scanning the sky for stars that would not show themselves.

"I can't think straight here," he said. "I feel confused and like I don't know what's real. Everything here seems so artificial. Everything. I can't survive in a place like this. I guess I'm more like that young man in buckskins than I ever thought."

"Don't go," she whispered, her heart breaking. To have come so close. He had actually said he loved her. And she had treated him as though he were a thief, a con artist, someone who could not be trusted.

"It wasn't you I didn't trust," she called as he walked away. "It was me."

His stride never faltered.

Spring was coming to Kootenay Lake. Little tufts of new green grass poked through old dead turf. The cedars and the grand firs smelled of new life and sported gentle green fronds of new growth.

Cole Standen sat on his deck, eyeing the moody waters of the lake. It was not possible, he decided, to call a bird onto your shoulder.

Still, they could be bribed as far as the railing of his deck. He laid out sunflower seed and called through his teeth.

A bird, one he had learned was called a purple finch, sashayed through the air, landed in front of him, eyed him warily, then dipped his head and took the seed.

A knock came on his door, and he glanced at his watch.

Some days, some of the kids came by after their video classes. There were two unspoken rules: one, their mother did not come with them; and two, they did not speak of Brooke.

"Come in," he called, then over his shoulder, as he heard the footsteps. "Saffron, watch this." He laid down the seed and whistled. The bird came, swooped down, stole the seed and was gone.

The gasp of pleasure made him look behind him. He scrambled from his chair.

"You can call the birds from their nests," she said.

"Sometimes. It's a trick. I bribe them." She looked beautiful. Thinner. Sadder, but beautiful.

"How's everything in Hollywood?" he said, aiming for a casual tone, though his heart was beating out of his chest.

"Good. The guy you recommended to work on *Spring in the Desert* is remarkable. He's not letting them get away with anything. The film is going to be a masterpiece. It's going to be true."

"Great," he said. He wondered why he said that, when all he could care about was the fact that she was standing here with him. He wondered why they were making small talk.

"The security guy is amazing, too. I got the third degree before I even got in the driveway."

"Great. Good." He took a deep breath. "So you're here for a visit?"

"No, I'm not. I'm here for good."

"Pardon?"

"I came to see if I could learn to call birds from trees. Light fires. Live with a difficult, prickly man."

"Nobody asked you!" he said.

She came toward him. "But you wouldn't say no, would you, to a woman learning to trust her own heart? To a woman learning to say yes to the only thing that's real in this whole wide world?"

She had come and was standing right in front of him, looking him directly in the eye.

There was something different about her.

A new confidence. A woman who had asked herself what she wanted and come up with an answer.

He had the utterly humbling feeling her answer might have been him.

She held out her hands, and he took them, gazed at her, pulled her in hard to him. "Welcome home," he said, and he swung her around until they were both breathless with laughter.

"It's not a game," he told her when he set her down. "You can't play until you're sick of it and then go home."

"I am home," she reminded him.

"We have to get married."

"I was hoping."

"Secretly. Absolutely no input from the dragon lady up there."

She laughed. "I was hoping that, too."

He stood back from her and looked at her. The most astonishing thing happened. It was as if all the world faded away, and all that was left was love.

The love that shone in her eyes.

The love that stirred in his heart.

Everything became the same. The love in his heart was the same force at the heart of that wild lake, the same force at the heart of those blades of grass, the same force unfurling in the new leaves on the trees.

For an astonishing, suspended moment he saw the truth. That love made him one with all things.

A bird, the little purple finch, circled them, and then, astoundingly, landed on his shoulder.

So, it was not getting the whistle right that called the

birds from the trees, and it was not bribing them with sunflower seeds.

It was love, all of creation humbled in the presence of this great power, the one that called the birds from the trees and the fish from the sea and that allowed a man to walk on water.

Ever so gently, Cole placed his finger under the finch's tiny, leathery feet. It hopped up, snapping onto his finger with surprising strength. He put out his arm, and the bird went to her shoulder, sidled up to it, pecked her on the cheek and then flew away.

"I do believe that your great-grandmother just kissed me on the cheek," she said, not even brushing at the tears that coursed down her face.

"I do believe you are right."

And then they turned and watched, hand in hand, as the sun sank, blazing, beyond still mountains, and the birdcalls died and the moon came out.

Together, they said goodbye to the day and hello to forever.

Epilogue

*T*ap. *Tap. Tap.*

"Don't let them in," Cole said. "Their mother sent them. You know what she wants, and she's not getting it."

Brooke threw back her head and laughed. On the first day he had ever seen her, he had caught a glimpse of beauty, but nothing could have prepared him for what she held within her.

A radiance of such proportions it could capture a man, make him want to spend whole days doing nothing but looking at her smile, her eyes, the cascade of chestnut hair falling down her back, the growing roundness of a belly.

"Get the door," she said, waving a wooden spoon at him. This week she was learning to make cookies. Last week it had been painting. The week before that she had taken up knitting. She had this enormous appetite for life, an eagerness to learn *everything*.

"Oh, sure," he grumbled. "Send your slave to get the door."

He opened it, crossed his arms over his chest and looked sternly at his visitors. No sense letting them see the smile he felt inside.

Saffron was not the least fooled by his expression. She reached up on tiptoe and kissed his cheek. "Hi, Uncle Cole."

A diversionary tactic. The rest of the little crew slipped right in his door and ran through to where Brooke was in the kitchen.

He came in and leaned on the door frame. They were gathered around her, peering dubiously into the bowl.

"I'm making cookies," she said. "Don't you think every mother should know how to make cookies?"

"I don't think our mother does," Darrance said slowly. "Auntie Brookie, cookies aren't the important part. The love is the important part."

From the mouths of babes, Cole thought. And the truth was, for all her faults, Shauna loved her children and Milton with a fierceness and devotion that were nothing short of awe-inspiring.

Milton, now *there* was a surprise. A man of wisdom and depth and gentleness, he had actually become one of Cole's closest friends. And Shauna? Once she decided you were worthy of her trust, she was more annoying than ever! Brooke and Cole were showered with a constant stream of unwanted gifts and advice.

But underneath all that was the important part. Somehow, Shauna's fierce love and devotion extended to them. With the baby coming, Shauna was in high gear. She had it in her head that she was naming the baby. She'd actually suggested Oscar, right after she had won one for *Spring in the Desert*.

"Oh, look what they've brought, Cole," Brooke said with delight, as if she hadn't been presented with the same thing nearly every single day since they had revealed to the Carrier clan they were expecting a baby.

"Name suggestions?" he guessed dryly. "Do you guys sit around your kitchen table at night dreaming up names?"

And what names, too! Zenobia. Talitha. Drusilla. Ackley. Maximillian. And those were the more ordinary ones.

"Yes!" Kolina said happily. "Mine." She toddled over and gave him her envelope. He opened it. In purple crayon it said XDTYPP.

"Exdeetip," he read. "Hmm. Better than Zenobia. What do you think, Brooke?"

Kolina grabbed the paper back from him and scowled at it. "Doesn't say that. Says Kolina. For a girl."

"No, Kolina, we all agreed," Saffron reminded her little sister. She handed an envelope to Brooke.

Good-naturedly Brooke opened it.

"Look, guys," he said. "Isn't it enough that you've taken over my beach? Do you have to name my baby?"

He heard a small noise from Brooke and looked over. A single tear rolled down her cheek.

"Cole?"

"Honey, what is it?" He was at her side in an instant.

"I think they've just named our baby."

He took the paper from her. It had, as always, two columns, one headed Girl and the other headed Boy. But instead of the usual array of impossible names, only two were there.

Eileen. James.

He had to bite his tongue against his own swell of emotion. For this is what he had learned in the amazing time he had been with Brooke: everything had its season. Everything lived and everything died. So why was it people continued to hope and dream and grow and learn?

Because love, that most mystic and powerful of all energies, love survived, like an arrow sent forward through the fabric of time.

Somehow the words to say all that evaded him, so instead he said, "Thank God it's not Oscar."

* * * * *

Don't miss Cara's next book,
HER SECOND-CHANCE MAN.
Available July 2004,
only from Silhouette Romance.

SILHOUETTE *Romance*®

presents

DADDY'S LITTLE MEMENTO
by Teresa Carpenter
(Silhouette Romance #1716)

**When Samantha Dell showed up
on Alex Sullivan's doorstep with
his chubby-cheeked baby in tow, she
never imagined Alex would want to
be a full-time parent—or her husband!**

Available April 2004 at your favorite retail outlet.

If you enjoyed what you just read,
then we've got an offer you can't resist!

Take 2 bestselling love stories FREE!

Plus get a FREE surprise gift!

SILHOUETTE *Romance*®

COMING NEXT MONTH

#1714 THE PIED PIPER'S BRIDE—Myrna Mackenzie
The Brides of Red Rose

The women of Red Rose needed men—and they'd decided sexy Chicago bigwig Parker Monroe was going to help find them! But Parker wasn't interested in populating his hometown with eligible bachelors. Enter their secret weapon, Parker's former neighbor. But how was the love-shy Ellie Donahue supposed to entice her former crush to save the town without sacrificing her heart a second time?

#1715 THE LAST CRAWFORD BACHELOR—
Judy Christenberry
From the Circle K

Assistant District Attorney Michael Crawford was perfectly happy being the last unmarried Crawford son and he didn't need Daniele Langston messing it up. But when Dani aroused his protective instincts, his fetching co-*worker* became his co-*habitant*. Now this business-minded bachelor was thinking less about the courtroom and more about the bedroom....

#1716 DADDY'S LITTLE MEMENTO—Teresa Carpenter

The only convenient thing about Samantha Dell's marriage was her becoming a stepmother to precious eleven-month-old nephew Gabe. Living with Gabe's seductive reluctant daddy didn't work into her lifelong plans. *And getting pregnant by him?* Well, that certainly wasn't part of the arrangement! Would falling in love with her heartthrob husband be next?

#1717 BAREFOOT AND PREGNANT—Colleen Faulkner

Career-driven Ellie Montgomery had everything a girl could want—except a husband! But *The Husband Finder* was going to change that. Except, according to the book, her perfect match, former bad-boy Zane Keaton, was definitely Mr. Wrong! But a few of Zane's knee-weakening, heart-stopping kisses had Ellie wondering if he might be marriage material after all.

SRCNM0304